WHY DOES THE SANE SOLDIER THINK HE IS A DOG?

AND OTHER STORIES

First published in the UK by Beacon Books and Media Ltd by arrangement with Kalemat Agency KSA.

Beacon Books and Media Ltd, Earl Business Centre, Dowry Street, Oldham OL8 2PF, UK.
www.beaconbooks.net
www.kalematagency.com

Why Does the Sane Soldier Think He Is a Dog? by Mohammed Al-Aradi was first published in Arabic by Kalemat Publishing House in Saudi Arabia 2020.

Cover design by Raees Mahmood Khan

T2822

WHY DOES THE SANE SOLDIER THINK HE IS A DOG?

AND OTHER STORIES

BY MOHAMMED AL–ARADI
TRANSLATED BY T.M. KIANI

BB
BEACON BOOKS

Dedication

To my friend, the poet Shadi Sami, who now rests in Al-Arish

He spent the years of his life studying the stars.

Contents

Crocodiles

Maybe I was afraid, or perhaps not, or could it have been anxiety that had rendered me reckless in temperament? I fear that something might drop upon me from above, shattering the bones of my skull. When that muffled explosive sound reverberated, I woke up suddenly, instinctively covering my head with my arms and murmured, "Something fell." I imagined I had fallen from the bed, and I reached to feel my head. The woman next to me screamed like someone fearing death; she remembered her brother who had entered the bathroom in winter... the water heater exploded. I think the echoes of that explosion continued to haunt him in his grave. Maybe he didn't die quickly and felt the melting of his scalp as he kicked in fury above the white, gleaming bathtub infused with the chlorine scent. Mother didn't always use chlorine. The woman sleeping next to me is not like Mother. She once recalled that in her younger days, she fell from a car seat. She fell from a car seat and onto the asphalt, scraping her buttocks and tearing her knees, harbouring a fear of the blood in her pants yet remained silent. Her uncle, who halted the car, scolded her and blamed her for not sitting properly... Why did she fall while the other children in the car did not fall from the car onto the asphalt and did not scrape their knees? Her uncle felt angry and seized her hand; he struck her with his grip.

I told the woman lying beside me that the maths teacher who carried a contraption in his clothes pocket would render it into two pieces, thrusting one half into his pocket; he would bring it out if the other did not provide the desired result. He would strike with an old belt, twisting his tongue and hitting. And if the child moved his hand away, he would hit him on the buttocks, on the back, the left thigh, the shin, the head; the skin of the buttocks does not tear, though it reddens. I am not regretful of anything, but afraid. They say that the Nile will run dry, and the tilapia will not find water. When asked about the 'bultim', I said that I didn't know, thinking that it was the name of a fish from those of the Nile that will not find water. But she, in her foolishness, said that 'bultim' was the name of a disease in proper Arabic, such as 'humaq' (chicken pox) which we call 'anqaz' (neck rash). 'Humaq' is a contagious disease, but that does not scare me like leprosy does, which appears on the hands and above the eyebrows. Though I have not suffered from any hereditary illnesses, my paternal grandmother struggled with dementia. She would plea, "Take the children away from me," even though there was no one with her. I forget, I become confused, and perhaps anxiety has rendered me reckless in my temperament. I become furious, sometimes, thinking of hitting her hard because she asks, "What happened?" and I do not want to answer. Why is it that we don't complain to the police? And this means that I am helpless and powerless.

When that muffled explosive sound echoed, I woke up suddenly, clutching onto my head. The sound had come from the bathroom. If the woman had fallen, we would surely have heard a sound much different than this – the sound of shattering glass. Inside the bathroom was a white plastic rack which I was not too fond of because of its evident lack of craftsmanship. Nevertheless, she had bought it because I was not prepared to pay for a wooden rack. We don't have a plastic fitted bathtub, nor a dull metal one – a bathtub we call 'Banyo'. In the bathroom is a European-style fitted toilet that allows even any obese woman to sit on, but she would soon begin to sweat as the bathroom is confined and the extractor fan is faulty. Perhaps the one who designed this tiny space had planned to make it a storeroom, originally, but then the house owner's wife came and decided to change it into a bathroom. When mother came, she remarked, "I cannot use an Arabic toilet." I myself sat on the Arabic toilet.

In the old days, each time I entered the bathroom at night, I would imagine a mysterious black hand extending from the toilet drainage hole, and, out of intense fear, I would imagine it touching me. Now that I am employed and have a wife, I am not afraid, even if I was to see a hairy monster in the bathroom staring right at me with its eyes, thinking that I would punch it in the abdomen, or skin it with half a contraption. I wrap the first blade over my hand and I grip it as hard as I can. I once suffered a severe headache, one that they write about in medical textbooks, and I wrapped a bandage around my head so tightly that I thought my skull would lose its shape. In the mirror in the bathroom, at first glance, I appear like a weary warrior, though I am more like a patient yearning for rest. During the days when my head was wrapped, I watched a film, a sickening one, and I thought it would affect my dreams.

The woman next to me was reading "The Crocodile" sto-ry, an unfinished tale written by Dostoevsky about Mr. Ivan Matveitch, who was swallowed by a crocodile, Karl, and his wife, because of it, let out a piercing scream. Her screams were supernaturally loud, but Mr. Ivan did not die but asked for police assistance from inside the crocodile's stomach. I read the stories of the saints as excellent tales of wonders. I read the in-cident of the crocodile abducting Mr. Mukhaymir Al-Naqib's daughter. I read that Mr. Mukhaymir Al-Naqib came crying to shaikh Al-Farghali, complaining about what had happened to his daughter, so he said to him, "Go to the place from which she was snatched and call out loudly: "O crocodile, come and speak to Al-Farghal."" He did as he was told, and the crocodile came out walking in the village, and the people followed until the crocodile stopped at the shaikh's door. The shaikh ordered the blacksmith to extract the crocodile's teeth, and the croc-odile remained silent, observing, saying nothing. When the blacksmith had finished, the shaikh said: "Remove the poor girl from your stomach," so it took her out, and she had turned insane because of what had happened to her. Then the shaikh took an oath from the crocodile not to snatch anyone from the village, so the crocodile shook its tail in agreement, and it shed tears. If the crocodile kidnapped my daughter or swallowed her without killing her, I would do as Ivan Matveitch had request-ed and seek help from the police. It occurred to me that the stubborn crocodile I saw in the zoo would not understand my words if I called out to it and said, "Come, let's negotiate." And perhaps if I thought a little further, I wouldn't ask for help from anyone; people have malicious intentions and wouldn't believe it even if we use X-rays.

When that muffled explosive sound echoed, I jumped from my slumber, my head heavy with drowsiness. Then I sat up. I wanted to sink back into the numbness of sleep beneath the covers, but the woman sleeping next to me foolishly exclaimed: "Thief." I became angered and got up to walk. Walking in the darkness is unsettling, as one might imagine seeing dark visions they perceive as demons. If I had taken a drink from the kitchen and remained there for a while before returning and saying to her, "I didn't find anything," she would have believed it. But I heard a faint whimper coming from the bathroom. The washing machine doesn't whine but emits a whirring sound. The bathroom light was on, and the electricity bill is expensive. When I opened the bathroom door, expecting to find a ghost, I saw a real man – short, heavily built, and with thick hair. I calmed myself and cursed him for startling me. I kicked the bathroom door to show him my anger, and I was prepared to punch him in the stomach because he was a thief. He covered himself with his arms and said, "I'm scared. Help me." He said they were chasing him and he couldn't find any way out, so he entered through the drainage hole – the drainage hole in the European-style toilet. I called him a liar and asked, "Are you trying to play tricks on me?" I angrily shouted at the woman who came behind me, and I didn't tell her to call the police. I felt confused and resentful. Why is this thief trying to rob us? I was afraid that he would notice my hesitation, so I told him to get up, and I slapped him hard – a slap so hard I didn't realise I was capable of. His head jerked, and I wanted to punch him hard in the stomach to make sure I wasn't hesitant. I led him to the storeroom, where I noticed that he was of small stature and his head resembled a cone, but I wouldn't believe for a moment that he had entered through the drainage hole because the drainage pipes are twisted. He didn't cry like the crocodile that snatched the daughter of Mukhaymir Al-Naqib, but was submissive, saying, "Help me." I threw him into the room and bound his hands and feet. I thought I was still in a dream, and that I would soon wake up to the sound coming from the bathroom. The woman didn't believe it, then she unknowingly said, "I told you he's a thief." Then she said, "This is from the influence of the long movies you watch." I hurried back to the storeroom because I hadn't closed the door, and I found the short man unbound, sitting humbly. If the woman sleeping next to me had seen me slapping him with that mighty strike that jolted his head, she would have thought differently and said that I am not defenceless. Then I remembered that the storeroom had become a bathroom, and we had installed a European-style toilet there because of mother's weak knee. Like any storeroom you can imagine, this storeroom was also dark and damp, and cluttered with damaged and obsolete items. The woman had put a sewing machine in there, and videotapes. I apprehended that he might have hidden a knife under him, and he might attack me with it, then assault the woman or hide in the house, so we wouldn't be able to find him without the help of the police. I thought to myself that if I can get him out of the house, I will be relieved of him and then I can go back to sleep; after all, I have work tomorrow and it's late. But if I told him to leave without hitting him, he would think I'm afraid or hesitant, and the woman would call me a coward, so I decided to approach him quickly and throw myself at him or kick him hard without pausing until he collapses. If I left him the chance, he would pull out the knife from under him. However, he said submissively, "Please, help me."

I pretended not to notice and didn't ask him about the restraint he had undone so he would think I hadn't realised. I told him, "Alright, I will forgive you, but don't think I'm incapable of burying you right here." He said, "I am not a thief. I couldn't find a way and entered through the drainage hole because they were chasing me." From among the dilapidated items, I picked up a wooden bat, and stepped back a little outside the dark store so that he could see me holding a solid bat. I asked him to move, to make sure he wasn't hiding a knife; if he was hiding a knife, I wouldn't forgive him, and I would crush his skull, and the police could do what they wanted. The short man, whose skull I might crush, had a shiny complexion and delicate hands, like a child's. When the woman saw him, she said, "He's not a thief; perhaps he's lost." He could be a noble person being pursued, who found safety in our bathroom." But how can I believe that he entered through the drainage hole in the bathroom when the drainage pipes are twisted? If he were to poke his head out of the drainage hole and wedge the rest of his body into the twisted drainage pipes, then I would believe it. A fierce storm swept over us, in the olden days, and hail fell on cars, tree branches, house roofs, trash cans, and even on the car bonnets until it dented them. My mother closed the windows, and my father said that his car's windows would shatter. The sound of the hail crashing down on everything would force you to raise your voice, like the noise of a loud party or the interference of a TV station. In that fierce storm, uncle found an Asian worker at the entrance of his house, and he was angry at him. The Asian worker didn't say that he was lost or that he had entered through the drain, but he said in broken language that he was afraid and wanted to take shelter from the hail, as it hit him hard on his head. Uncle saw blood on the worker's shirt. Though he was angry, he left him waiting at the house entrance and then told him, "Get out." I told the man whom I initially thought was a thief, "Get out," but he didn't leave, and he said, "They are waiting for me. You are a good man. Help me." I thought that he is now trying to play me, so I struck him hard with the wooden bat I was holding in my hand, causing him to moan like a dog in the cold, with blood pouring from his head.

"Who are those chasing you?"

"I don't know," he said, as he winced from the blow's impact.

I felt a sense of relief because I had hurt him, and I thought to myself, "If he were a thief, he would have pulled out the knife and attacked me." The woman thought he was handsome – although she didn't express it – because the lighting in the storeroom was dim, and she said, "Let's take him as an example for the children."

"I will bury him in the storeroom," I said to her. "There are many houses. Why did he enter my house? Did he think I couldn't force him out?"

The man overheard our conversation and said, "I'm not a teacher, but I can cultivate the land."

You, dear reader, might say, "None of this happened, and I am writing a story about the Israelis, and the man who entered my bathroom through the drainage hole is a metaphor for the entry of the Haganah gangs into Arab neighbourhoods in Haifa." But you are mistaken, my dear friend, and let's assume that I fabricated the story of the man in the bathroom, and that the story is a metaphor as you say. I'll happily join you in this imagination which I have no idea whence you brought, how a wooden bat in my hand resembles the British and French rifles – remnants of World War I – held by Arab volunteers, whose number was no more than 450 in Haifa under the leadership of Amin Izzuddin Al-Lubnani, the sole member of the Arab Liberation Army, led by a Palestinian public health engineer with no military experience. How could it resemble a single submissive man – whom I had slapped with force – who entered the bathroom of my house through the drainage hole, compared to 3,000 organised fighters in the Carmeli Brigade, who had armoured vehicles, 2-inch and 3-inch howitzers, machine guns, rifles, hand grenades, homemade rocket launchers firing shells weighing 60 pounds, or oil drums packed with explosives, rolling them down from high areas onto the Arab neighbourhoods below? And how could it resemble a short man who entered my bathroom through the drainage hole, without executing any armed operation against me, unlike the armed gangs that executed the Operation Bi'ur Hametz – Hametz means 'removing leavened bread from Jewish homes during the Passover holiday – as a protest against Arab citizens with the intention of killing them and expelling them. And how a frightened man kneeling down in submission, pleading: "Help me," resembles armed gangs, attacking Arab areas in Haifa on three fronts, on a Wednesday morning, from north of the old market, south of the municipal hall, and from the direction of Wadi Rushmia Bridge, to cut off the path of families attempting to escape the mortar shells. If we were to overlook these matters, how do you think, my dear friend, I would have fabricated a story and turned a bathroom with a European-style toilet into a metaphor for Haifa? There is nothing true here that you had thought, and nothing about the Haganah even crossed my mind. I only wrote about what happened in my bathroom, and that too exactly how it occurred without any exaggeration. I am not like Dostoevsky or Abdulwahhab Al-Sha'rani. I merely wanted to write about what happened without embellishments. Anyhow, this false notion filled me with anger – that the reader thought that I was writing about the Israelis. As such, when the man said, "I can cultivate the land," I swung at him with the wooden bat in my hand, seeking to slit open him belly and expose his intestines. Instead, I struck his wide back with a violent blow instead. He stooped like a wounded man bending his body, and I felt sorry for him. The woman said, "Enough." I felt glad because the woman saw the powerful blow. However, I was somewhat embarrassed because the man who entered my bathroom through the drainage hole became weak, moaning like a wounded person and not speaking, looking confused. I told him without showing any embarrassment. I told him without hindrance, "For the sake of this woman." He said, without hesitation, "I am not a thief. They were chasing me and I found no other way so I came in through the drainage hole." He reached into his coat pocket and took out some money, saying, "I'm not a thief." The woman thought to herself, "This handsome man cannot be a thief," and she believed him. I did not believe him entirely, and thought to myself, "Maybe he lost his way." I told him, "I won't involve the police, and I'll let you go. But if you enter my house through the bathroom drainage hole again, I will bury you in the bathroom. Do you understand what I am saying?"

However, he turned to me and said submissively, "I will not leave."

When I recounted this story to the woman sleeping next to me, she didn't say it's a story about Israelis. She said, "This is the influence of crocodile stories on you." In the evening, the woman heard a muffled explosion and screamed of someone fearing death, exclaiming, "The Haganah gang!" I imagined myself falling from the bed, felt around for my head, and thought to myself, "But our bathroom isn't in Haifa."

Life in the Slow Clerk's Office

When Mr. S woke up one morning from disturbing dreams, he found himself transformed into a monstrous insect in his bed, much like what happened to Gregor Samsa. However, he realised he needed to get up from his bed and head to the Civil Affairs Office to complete a simple procedure.

When Mr. S stumbled upon the gate under the watchful eye of the security guard who was smoking a damp cigarette he had taken from the Communications Department employee, everything in the Civil Affairs Office seemed to be proceeding as usual. The reception area was crowded with heads and shoes as well. Mr. S stood there, stooped, checking his papers, then sat on the edges of his fingers, placing his plastic document holder on the ground, and began arranging his documents. He stood in line like people usually do in the queue of waiting visitors. The old man, who was waiting for someone to tell him that he was tired of standing, said to him, "I've been standing still for a long time because of this leisurely clerk," Mr. S nodded his head in agreement. The old man told him that his son-in-law works as a clerk at the Civil Affairs Department but in another city, and if he worked here, he would have sorted everything out in no time. Mr. S said, "Ah... exactly," and slid his left hand into his coat pocket, looking at him with disdain.

When it was the turn of the old man who was standing in front of Mr. S, the clerk asked him for his appointment paper, but he didn't know anything about it, so the clerk told him that he couldn't assist him, "I'm sorry, sir, you need to schedule an appointment." The old man explained that he was elderly and unfamiliar with such procedures, asking the clerk to be lenient with him. When the old man's desperation grew, he said to the clerk:, "My daughter's husband works with you. He is the head of the Archives Department. Please help me." The clerk explained to him that bypassing the system for any reason was impossible. Mr. S presented his documents to the clerk and explained what he wanted, observing the movement of the clerk's fingers on the keyboard. After about the seventeenth movement, the employee returned Mr. S's documents, saying, "I'm sorry, sir, I can't assist you. The system shows that you are deceased, and we cannot serve a deceased person; your file is closed." Mr. S furrowed his eyebrows in alarm and pushed his head back, looking at the clerk with a sense of inquiry, as if questioning something obscure, "I apologise, but I can't do anything. Your death is registered in the system," said the clerk as he pointed his finger towards the 'death section' in the form displayed in front of him. Mr. S felt like this was a silly joke that would quickly end, "What are you saying? How can I be deceased while I am standing in front of you at this very moment? This is unreasonable." The clerk said, "Look," and scrolled the screen to allow Mr. S to see the date of his death. Mr. S wiped his hands with his coat, "But I am not deceased. I'm standing right before you as you can see." He said in frustration, "I don't know why you don't believe what you see with your own eyes. You are getting on my nerves. Obviously, there must have been a mistake."

"The system data is completely accurate. If you want to correct your data, you need to apply to amend it and bring along a certificate from the court and a medical report."

The clerk signalled to the next person in line, indicating for Mr. S to step aside. "If you insist that you're not dead, go back to the Registry Department and discuss this matter with them."

Mr. S retreated and refused within himself to believe that what happened was real. Then he became aware of the overlapping voices in the reception hall and wanted to hit the clerk. Then he said to himself, "The fault is his own," because he could not convince the clerk despite the issue being very clear, and he realised that he was unable to speak using the fewest words to prove that: 'I had not died yet'. Then he added, "Everything happened so quickly, therefore, it was not possible to clarify the triviality of the matter."

He sat on the iron waiting chairs, making sure he hadn't lost any of his documents. The man sitting next to him tried to tell him something, pointing to the ground, but Mr. S didn't notice. After a quick review of what had happened, he decided that it wasn't worth going to court or obtaining a medical report. He was capable of proving that he hadn't died whenever he met an employee of a rank higher than this completely incompetent one.

The hair on the clerk's cheek was annoying to any who saw it, and Mr. S felt a terrible discomfort and wanted to remove it. The clerk held a magnifying glass, observing a set of letters, making sure of their linguistic formulation. Mr. S stood in front of the desk and succinctly explained his problem in a confused manner, saying he didn't know how it happened. The clerk raised the magnifying glass and examined Mr. S's face, then placed it down. "What a situation! Don't you see I'm busy? You must think that we have nothing to deal with apart from your issue. Why don't you wait until I ask you to come in? Doesn't your behaviour express a lack of manners?" Mr. S didn't know if he wanted an answer or if it was a rhetorical question, but he responded nonetheless, "Ah... yes." "Please don't speak until I finish what I am saying," said the clerk, "What a lack of manners people have these days!" The clerk then said, "You have a problem, huh? Let me, with over thirty years of experience as a clerk, tell you that you are the cause of the problem." The clerk stood up from his chair and continued, "I know what you are going to say: that this system is complicated and overly intricate. That's because you're a bunch of malicious individuals who possess the greatest degree of stupidity."

Mr. S wanted to respond to this insult and clarify to him that he was not one of those malicious individuals who possessed the greatest degree of stupidity, and that he respected the system, but he felt a sense of dread before this impassioned speech. "Ah... that's true, but not always, sir," he said with a fragmented voice. "Not always?! This is the best thing I could hear this morning. If it is as you say it is, then why don't you complete your request and bring the rest of the necessary documents? What do you lose by following the system? If you're asked to bring a paper, a photo, a contract, or a certificate from any source, why don't you bring these documents? If you're asked to jump, sit, or hit your own cursed self with your shoe...

even if you don't understand the benefit of this request, do it while being assured that the system is designed for the benefit of everyone."

Mr. S realised that he had made a mistake by involving himself in matters that didn't concern him. "I have brought everything requested of me, but my problem, sir, as I told you, is that I am registered in the system as deceased, yet here I am. This is the issue." Mr. S wanted to add, "It happened because of one of the employees," but he feared implicating himself in another problem.

The clerk, thinking that Mr. S had not understood what he had previously said, stated, "The fact that you are registered as deceased in the system means you are indeed deceased, and that is what matters. You must understand that here we only deal with what is in your file," the clerk continued, tapping on the table. "What is written in your papers, you must deal with that yourself. We cannot believe anyone who claims something without providing evidence for it, otherwise all matters would become complicated and out of control."

Mr. S responded with annoyance, "But you know, sir, that I am not deceased, and there must have been a mistake."

"It appears that you don't understand. Whether you are dead or a stray dog, it doesn't matter. What's important is what is recorded in your file. Right now, you are listed as deceased, and if you do not want to act like a dead person and want to make any changes, you need to provide authenticated proofs with official stamps, not just claim whatever you want in front of the staff because that doesn't mean anything. In your case, you need to fill out Form No. 45 clearly, and provide a certificate from the judiciary and a medical report from any government hospital. We do not accept reports issued by private hospitals. I also warn you, if you try to cause trouble, your matter will be dealt with. Now tell me, is everything clear?" Before he could respond, the clerk added, clarifying, "If someone passes away, do they come and tell us, 'Hey, you guys, I died yesterday, and you need to adjust my data?' Things don't work that way. Instead, one of their relatives comes with documents stamped with official seals, and then everything is resolved smoothly, and no one has a problem."

"Ah… that's true, but none of my relatives have brought the documents confirming my death," replied Mr. S. The clerk responded angrily, "Let me give you an example. Do you know what an example is? It's just an example." He nodded towards the door, "Come on, don't waste my time. The process is easy, but you're complicating it for yourself by not understanding. You will make your life difficult if you go on like this."

Here, I want to note an observation about the unjustified reaction of this clerk, who seemed to be agitated because Mr. S entered without permission. In reality, as I later discovered, this clerk was preoccupied with forging a promotion letter for a dismissed employee. Perhaps this clerk was a secretary in his office. The agitated clerk coordinated with the other employees, one of whom works in the Human Resources Department and the other in the Finance Department, not to submit a letter to the general management regarding the dismissal of the editorial secretary, and to cover up this matter. This allows the Finance Department to continue paying the dismissed secretary's salary, and then the three share his salary, with a higher percentage going to the employee working in the Finance Department. Therefore, when Mr. S entered the office, the clerk felt anger and frustration because he was confirming the format of the forged letter, at that moment, being written in the name of the dismissed secretary, requesting a promotion to a higher rank. The clerk was cautious of making a mistake—whether in the wording, the content of the letter, or in some of the indications mentioned in the letter—that could expose their scheme. Anyway, no one cared why the clerk was so agitated, and the matter ended with the departure of Mr. S from the office disappointed, sensing a person who felt panicked about being involved in a dubious affair.

As he exited, Mr S. found someone standing in front of him, who said, "Please come with me." Mr. S felt an immense sense of trust emanating from this person, assuming he was an employee at the Civil Affairs Department, wanting to resolve the matter or inquire about some things regarding the mistake that occurred, and thus he should not resist him. As they walked through a corridor that hadn't been there before, Mr. S noticed that the ceiling of the corridor hadn't been painted yet. He said to the man who seemed to be leading him after stopping, "Ah... I want to be honest with you: I'm not comfortable with where we're going." Then he realised he had made a mistake in deciding to follow him: "I don't want any action to be taken regarding the mistake that occurred." He turned back and said firmly, "I want to leave; I'm late." The person he thought was an employee responded in a calm and confident voice, "You are subject to a simple procedure, a completely legal procedure, in compliance with the directives and letters received from the General Administration. Please come with me." And he extended his hand indicating for Mr. S to advance.

Continuing their walk through the corridor, they stopped in front of a wooden door that was peeling at the bottom due to stifling dampness. The person said to Mr. S, "Wait here and don't move." He entered the office and closed the door. Mr. S caught fragments of some words that didn't indicate anything, causing him confusion. He remained standing in front of the door, even when the employee was delayed for more than half an hour, he still did not change his position. He thought to himself, "This time they won't get the better of me. I'll stick to exactly what he says, giving no answers other than short and precise ones." Despite this disciplined idea that often saved him from many troubles, he still felt tense or uncertainty. He tried to remember if he had ever been in a similar situation before, but he failed to recall anything comparable. Everything in the corridor was silent as if it didn't exist, and this void was only broken by the sound of the employee calling Mr. S as he opened the office door, "The committee members are wait-ing for you." When Mr. S entered the office, he found three formally dressed employees sitting behind a steel desk, each with a nameplate in front of them that read 'Deputy Assistant Director-General for Registry Affairs, Director of the General Management Consultancy in the Audit Department,' and so on, all squeezed in tiny lettering that were barely readable be-cause the plates were so small, with the employee's name writ-ten after the job description. Anyway, who cares to read this nonsense while in this cold office with the cement floor resem-bling a bad cell? The employee ushered Mr. S forwards until he stopped him right in front of the desk. There were a set of reports on the desk, some handwritten and others printed. There was a yellow file with Mr. S's full name written on it, along with three blue pens, a hole puncher, a ruler about 10 cm long, a black eraser with a white tip, and some blank white papers. Meanwhile, as I describe what's on the desk to you, the employee who walked with Mr. S had entered through a door behind the three employees. When he closed it, the employee sitting in the middle asked Mr. S, "What's your name?" Mr. S hesitated, wiped his palms together, and glanced at the name written on the file to make sure he was saying his name as it was written. When he pronounced his name correctly, the employee replied, "Good." He then wrote something on a small piece of paper that he held in his hand and began reading the data in the file: National ID Number, Name, Date of Birth, Place of Birth, etc. Each time, Mr. S confirmed that the data was correct until he reached the eye colour: brown. Mr. S replied, fearing another mistake, "I'm not sure right now." The employee raised his head, "How can you not know, huh?" Mr. S replied submissively, "Oh, I meant I'm not sure." Well, can you tell me why you're not deceased as recorded in your file?" When Mr. S heard this question, he was filled with a terrible disgust, wanting to kick these fools. He had never seen anyone more foolish than them in his life. But he asked himself to be more composed. He wanted to show them with a few words that didn't carry broad meanings that what happened was just a mistake by one of their employees. However, he was overcome with fear, afraid they might catch something they could use against him. "Ah, honestly, I don't know, sir." The employee said to him, "Well, you should know next time." He opened the door and the employee who brought Mr. S to this office entered. He took Mr. S by the hand, who responded submissively, walking through a long corridor. After passing many closed office doors, they stopped at the door of an office at the end of the corridor. The employee asked Mr. S to enter and lie down on the floor, and Mr. S complied as the employee had requested of him. He entered the office and lay on his back, with every movement of his legs or arms, he looked at the employee standing at the door of the office and asked, "Like this?" and the employee signalled in approval.

The office was empty except for a few old files and scattered papers strewn across the floor, along with some stacked crates piled on top of each other. When the employee closed the office door, Mr. S lay on his back with alertness and caution, ensuring he didn't make any further foolish mistakes.

The Aftermath of a Car Accident

She pondered, almost without realizing, with any sense of sorrow, as if she were a depressed beetle, like the beetle she had crushed once against a window frame, realizing that perhaps it was her who had been crushed against it. This took place on Rainfield Street in front of the pawnshop she had just left, not paying attention to her surroundings, replaying in her mind what little money she had remaining. She couldn't shake off the image of the careless carriage, pulled by horses, one of them wheezing due to asthma, who was at that moment running, afraid of the lash of the drunk coachman who yelled at it, "I will show you how to be a racehorse!"

She opened her eyes to the fine lines and small gaps in the wooden sides of the carriage. Then she noticed the dampness on the horse's hooves. She almost fainted before she fell to the ground. She saw the blurry figure of the man who closed the window and then turned off the light on the third floor above Anderson's Cigar Shop, and heard the sound of him stretching on the bed. She expected him to do something before he fell asleep, but she didn't know what he was supposed to do. She remembered that her son hadn't slept in two years, because he was dead. She then asked, "How can the dead sleep?" She corrected herself, remembering that her son was killed in the riots instigated by the workers. She thought that if he were still working as a lubricant worker in the ship repair workshop, her situation would be better. Then she remembered that he had stolen from her twice. She said that if he stole from her a third time, she might become a depressed beetle. Then she said, "Why did I think of a depressed beetle?" She tied this thought to an old fear, a fear she didn't understand.

However, it's a trivial fear, like being afraid you might have forgotten to close a jar of red currant jam. She gets up from her bed to make sure, then curses herself, saying she's sick. She hears the sound of the water faucet in the bathroom, the sound of the water faucet turning. She saw the man who closed the window and then turned off the light, opened the window, and didn't turn on the light. His sight compelled her to say that she's dying now. The last time she received condolences was when her husband died, and she didn't feel any sorrow then either. She thought she would find peace after his death, but this expectation had never materialised for anyone. A large grey rat passed by her head, stopped, looked at her, and then continued running. She said, "There is no large grey rat with burn marks on its back in my kitchen." She heard the sound of the rat's claws scratching against the granite stone that paved the road and said, "It's eerie if it continues." Then everything went silent, and she expected to have died. Then, the short lamppost, which had been flickering on and off, went out. She asked why she had lived this life, then begged the Lord not to let her die, even if He deprived her of all worldly pleasures. She looked towards a shop advertisement for Ghalasky Pierre – that is how she read the name – installed on the ground, depicting three young women wearing short dresses and cloth hats inspired by French fashion. Then she reconsidered the meaning of worldly pleasures and failed to reach anything beyond her thoughts about a good family life. She remembered that when she looked again at the girl drawn on the left of the advertisement, she hadn't used any makeup except once. She asked the merciful Lord to return her to how she used to be. She felt a warm, heavy trickle pouring onto the bone of her thigh. She stretched out her hand slowly, saw dirt on the tips of her fingers, withdrew her hand, and said it was from pressing the coins too hard. After that, she slowly extended her hand, felt some blood and raised threads from her dress that had torn due to the fall. She thought she was about to die, but, within herself, she wanted to live, even it was for merely another half an hour. She sensed a strange taste in her mouth, so she spat on the ground, and saliva stretched from her mouth to the ground in the form of a thin thread. She said, "This is fresh blood." Then she wondered how blood could be so fresh. She heard the laughter of the woman entering the Deluxe Cinema now. She doubted the value of her life, and then remembered the humiliation she received from her husband as he raised a beer bottle and spilled some on his summer shirt. He was sitting in the living room while she was washing some dishes in the kitchen, and she heard him say that her face resembled a horse's testicle. Then she laughed at the comparison and said, "Death is bad in any case." She wanted to live even if her face did resemble a horse's testicle, but she couldn't bring herself to say that. She noticed the dampness on her back and said, "I'm sweating." Then she recounted that her elbow had dislocated when she was nine years old, and her mother scolded her severely; she re-membered it vividly as if it were happening in front of her right now. Her mother struck her forcefully on her right shoulder, "Why weren't you paying attention? You almost broke your neck," she said, not understanding the connection between the elbow and the neck. She cried and her hands sweated. She stretched her leg, trying to figure out if she had extended it to the appropriate position or not. A cold shiver ran through her body after her right foot touched the tram rail. She thought someone would soon help her. A smell of roasted lamb meat wafted from a nearby place. She said, "Damn it! I'm not sick, just confused." Then she panicked when she thought she might die right now, "What will I do in the grave all day – trapped and buried in the dirt?" Then she no longer paid attention to the smell of roasted lamb meat emanating from a nearby place. She saw the mouth of the drunken coachman who hit her, moving slowly, opening and closing, but she couldn't hear anything he said. She saw splatters of saliva flying, noticed his moustache quivering, and a black piece stuck between his front teeth. "I am going to die anyway, but please not now," she said, without directing her plea to anyone specific. Then she heard a voice without discerning whether it was the voice of the drunken coachman, the voice of the devil inside her, or the voice of her husband, "When the time comes that you deem appropriate, you will say again, 'Not now.'" When she heard that, she saw the policeman turning at the end of the street from the north, he turned and entered Gordon Street. She noticed a dark spot at the edge of his trousers, thinking it was a grease stain. Then she felt numbness in her leg again, and she remembered that she had never thought about death before, at which she was surprised. Then she heard the sound of a rat's claws scratching against the stone, but she didn't see it, and she wanted to live, even if she remained lying on the ground hearing the rat's claws scratching against the granite stone. Without uttering a word, she said to herself, "I will return to the pawnshop and leave, and no carriage will ever hit me again." Then she saw the mouth of the drunken coachman, and the voice suddenly erupted, "Where the hell did you come from?" He spat on her and tried to kick her. But the fat man in the pawnshop had rushed out when his customer, whom he was watching out of boredom as she left, was hit by the speeding carriage. He told her she wasn't injured and tried to help her up.

My Grandmother Salma's Dog

My grandmother's dog died at least twenty years ago. When we recall the details that my grandmother sometimes remembers and sometimes forgets, we might say that twenty years is just a joke or an open disregard for the chronicle of a dog merely because it is a dog. This sudden prejudice comes from the human who believes they have the right to dominate everything, even the sympathetic dog. My grandmother remembers that he died when she was forty years old, which means he died almost thirty years ago, which is a very long time for the memory of an elderly woman who is over seventy years of age. Therefore, we shouldn't trust her account too much, especially since she changes something in the narration each time.

To you, Hadban is just a dog, just a sheepdog. And if I tried to convince you with some stories, we might come up with a better phrase like: just a smart dog guarding the sheep. Anyway, people usually tend to diminish the significance of anything that doesn't relate to or represent themselves. On the contrary, we idealise things we consider a part of ourselves in one way or another. This is just how it is, even though some of us try to evade it.

To my grandmother, Hadban is the 'man of the house' or something close to that, and I think that she often goes beyond this meaning, though I cannot declare that, at least not in the presence of my father, and my uncle who handles the matter very sensitively. Such a statement could be considered a personal insult to my grandfather and the family in general. My grandfather passed away early in age, leaving my grandmother with my father, who wasn't my father yet. He had joined the military as a young man and moved to work in the south on the border with Yemen. Government jobs at that time were considered the pinnacle of glory that any person could acquire, with decent salaries and social status that my father even used on days away from work; he wouldn't accept any interaction less than the respect accorded to a military man. My uncle, with his thick moustache, spent most of his time stroking it and cursing people, mocking everything in an annoyingly incurious manner. He left my grandmother and went to work at Jeddah Port, as he says, but anyone who sees him would be certain that he's involved in some job less than honourable. The last member of the family, Hadban, is the only one who had been with my grandmother all the time since she took him from her aunt. He was a small puppy until the last night of his life. He used to help in herding the sheep and greeted guests with a special bark, chasing after their cars, which rarely passed by. What's remarkable is that he distinguished between people who were related to my grandmother and those who were not. At night, he guarded the mud house and the sheep pen while listening to my grandmother's singing. The village was full of dogs for the need in assistance in herding sheep, but Hadban was not just a smart sheepdog; he was Salma's friend from day one, and it was due to the harsh weather and his young age that my grandmother used to let him into the house, and perhaps when the cold intensified, she would cover him with some of her own old clothes.

My grandmother remembers that when Hadban became too dirty to tolerate, she took him to a small, abandoned pond and gestured to him with her hand and voice, hoping he would bathe himself naturally. She was nervous and afraid someone might see her, but Hadban, not understanding this tension, wagged his tail contentedly. After enduring for a long time, she grabbed him by the ear and dragged him into the pond. He stood there, looking at her, barking sharply. She struck him fretfully on his head and began lifting water with her hand, pouring it over his body, while with her other hand, she wiped the sweat from her forehead. She says that after some hesitation, she started to pass her hand over his back in surprise, saying, with a laugh, "I felt he was like my son."

As Hadban grew older, things changed, and he started spending his nights crouching between the house and the pen. He barked in response to distant and intermittent wolf cries and chased after shadows, behaving like a young recruit on his last day of military training. You could sense that he was enthusiastic and took things seriously, even when his eyesight failed him in his old age, he ran vigorously and in multiple directions, but he would quickly collide with a rock or stumble over a bush. My grandmother says that in his old age, he lost his mind and became restless, barking and running without focus or a specific goal. I think he wanted to hide his weakness after losing his eyesight.

Matters were pressing on normally, in the expected manner for the life of a solitary bedouin grandmother. She, with due patience, tended to her sheep, cooked with the addition of herbs whose taste she knew well from her experience, and waited a lot. However, she didn't wait for anything specific. She would mumble simple prayers, asking that everything remain as it is, addressing Allah as if He were a friend with a spontaneous bedouin dialect. She would call out to Hadban with an enthusiastic voice if she wanted him to exert extra effort, and then, as the sun approached evening, she would place water for him under the lote tree; Hadban always lay beneath it or in front of the door.

My grandmother recalls that on one occasion after sunset, with twilight lingering as she stood by the pen, she imagined seeing Hadban as a black figure. She returned to the pen to check on it, saying: "And as I returned, I heard a loud commotion and saw the sheep splitting into two groups, with a huge black figure moving between them. I lifted my dress and ran, barely reaching the pen before a grey wolf with thick fur and yellow eyes darted out from inside, holding a small kid between its jaws. It wasn't the first time I had seen a wolf, but this time it felt terrifying. Until that time, I had never felt like a lone woman as I did in that moment. Everything happened so quickly, much like the wolf's escape. I wasn't entirely clear-headed, or else I wouldn't have chased after it. I wouldn't have wasted all that time after it had gone, searching the ground around me for something useful, like a stone. The image of Hadban flashed in my mind, and I resumed running, calling out, "Hadban... Hadbaaan, help... The wolf has attacked!" He had already noticed what was happening and came running, kicking up dust behind him. I gestured with my hands towards the direction the wolf had gone, seeing its dark figure shrinking in the distance. Hadban ran, and I chased after him until I was tired. The distance between me and Hadban began to increase. I had to be with Hadban, but I couldn't carry on. Instead, I screamed at him as if I were a mother calling out to her child with certain fear, "Come back, Hadban... Hadbaan!" But Hadban continued to run until he disappeared into the night that had covered the area with its darkness."

My grandmother says: "I sat in front of the house, waiting, perhaps hoping he would return. Eventually, I was overcome with sleep, and I dozed off in my place. I dreamt that Hadban were a young and enthusiastic man carrying an old rifle, and I was sitting beside him helping him load the gunpowder. We were in a high place, but it wasn't a hill, and in front of us was a rocky outcrop where we had taken cover, and below this place were piles of stones shaped like battlements. Wolves armed with rifles were hiding behind them, but they were exposed to us. They were exchanging gunfire with us, and I occasionally signalled to Hadban when a wolf appeared in a way that allowed us to easily kill it, and Hadban never missed the opportunity. Whenever the gunpowder ignited, a wolf would drop dead, and the dream was filled with smoke and the sound of gunpowder exploding, and the bodies of the wolves. I woke up late at night covered in dust. I shook off my black robe, stood up, and looked towards Hadban's resting place under the lote tree, but could not find him. I went to the pen and didn't find him there either. I checked the place hoping he might be nearby, but there was no trace of him. Even after calling out loudly and searching in several directions, no one appeared. I went inside to rest on my bed, feeling anxious, thinking about the dream and about Hadban who had never previously disappeared like this or fought with wolves before. He used to content himself with chasing them and barking. I remained in this state until dawn came. I hurriedly got up and headed towards the mountain without any plan, hoping to find Hadban. I walked slowly, following Hadban's trail on the ground, following it until I reached a place close to the mountain. The place around me was deserted except for some bushes standing lazily under the sun's rays. I found traces of a scuffle, and I could distinguish at least one trace of Hadban and a wolf, along with some blood. I didn't know if it was Hadban's blood or that of a young kid. I glanced around in all directions, advanced a little, and raised my voice, calling out with my hands around my mouth: 'Hadbaaan... Hadbaaan!' lowering my voice slightly in hopes of hearing his bark. I scanned all around, up the mountain and down among the large rocks. I hadn't yet completed the third call when he emerged from behind a large boulder and barked at me softly. I rushed towards him: 'I hope you're okay, Hadban,' I said as he limped slowly towards me. I sat down, and he approached, wagging his tail. Fear and fatigue were obvious on him. I ran my hands over his body, lifting them whenever I felt something to check and ensure there was no blood on them. Then I examined the leg he was lifting, not putting weight on it, to reassure myself about his injury. I was relieved to find that there were no wounds. I indicated to him that we should go back, but he resisted and grabbed the edge of my garment in his mouth, pulling me toward the rock he had emerged from. I followed him until we reached it, and I couldn't believe what I saw: the kid goat curled up on itself, breathing heavily and with a low, strained sound, indicating pain, with some wounds that might take several days to heal. I picked up the kid goat and signalled for Hadban to return. He started walking in front of me, and I scolded him all the way: 'You won't catch the wolf again, Hadban.' When I reached home, I placed the kid goat inside and poured water for Hadban, who lay near the door, and I sat watching him. I saw a happiness in his eyes, a happiness I had never seen before."

My grandmother doesn't remember Hadban on account of it being a long story that begins when she acquired him from her aunt and ends with his death. Instead, she recalls Hadban in a fragmented way, each event having its own specific history. To her, there is no point in narrating the daily life details of a dog she received without crafting a meaningful story from it: Hadban jumped a metre and a half, scratched his head for the first time, Hadban's preference for undercooked meat, etc. do not seem significant on their own, but these initial details might not accumulate into a meaningful end. This meaning is what my grandmother understands, even if it's not apparent to her in those details. Humans only tell stories to express a meaning, and that is why no one knows what happened during the time that passes swiftly in my grandmother's memory between rescuing the young goat and the incident of his death. In fact, she never mentioned to anyone how Hadban became blind. But it's certain that nothing significant happened, at least not according to Grandma, else she would have narrated a story about it, or perhaps this period was short and passed quickly. If the issue of Hadban's blindness was significant, then perhaps his blindness came from the natural gradual deterioration, for a man grows old, experiences health issues, his hearing becomes weak, and then one distant day, he realises that he can't see well, and so on and so forth. This gradual degradation doesn't allow blindness to be shocking enough to have its own story.

Anyway, these are my own interpretations, and the matter could be entirely different. My grandmother says, "When Hadban grew older, he became blind and relied entirely on his sense of smell and acute hearing. I began to watch over Hadban anxiously as I went about my chores. From time to time, I would raise my head and look at him, fearing he might hurt himself, so I would alert him with sound if he encountered anything he could bump into. Nevertheless, Hadban became depressed and irritable. At the mere sound of a distant noise, he would rush peevishly, barking in various directions and moving quickly with sudden turns, perhaps preparing for a fight as if he was seeing ghosts before him. He would remain in this state until I called out to him. Since he was afflicted with blindness, he could no longer guard the flock at night. When night falls, I bring him inside to sleep, and in the morning, he herds the sheep with me, following the sound of the flock wherever I go or my singing voice.

It was on one cold night when I went to check the pen to make sure everything was okay that I found that a large cover, which I had fixed on the window to block the cold wind, had a part of it come loose. As for the opposite side, I had placed several wooden panels. I lifted the loose part and tied it tightly this time. I held the cover and pulled it forcefully to ensure its firmness, with Hadban standing beside me motionless. He didn't move until I called him to return to the house. I gave him water and tapped the dish to let him know its location. I stood by the door until he drank, then we went inside. It was a quiet day like any other. I slipped into my bed after covering Hadban with a worn, long cloth to keep him warm and fell asleep. I was startled from my sleep by his barking loudly. I heard the sound of him colliding with the door. The sound stopped for a moment but then returned with him barking more fiercely. I hurriedly rushed out, chasing after him and calling out to him. The darkness was thick, covering everything. I tripped and fell, and I think I may have injured myself then. I got up and followed the sound of Hadban, which was gradually fading away and coming from multiple directions. I stumbled in the darkness of the night, seeing nothing but fleeting black shapes moving and disappearing swiftly, stirring up dust. I distinctly remember hearing the howling of two or more hyenas, but everything was mixed up and distant, and I couldn't make out what was happening. I was calling out to Hadban and hearing intermittent squealing and barking from various nearby directions. It was as if I was in the midst of a whirlwind, nothing seemed as it should.

Gradually, the sounds faded into the distance, and the darkness returned silent except for the movement of the dark figures and the clear whistling of the wind through the trees. The air grew colder, and I hugged myself, calling out, "Hadban!" but I heard no bark. I returned home after waiting in vain for a response, feeling the unbearable cold. I couldn't sleep until the sun spread its light, and then I ventured out, trying to reach the place where I thought I had heard Hadban's bark. I found traces of where I had fallen and the thorns I stumbled over. Near me, I saw traces of Hadban, and the area in front of me was filled with intermittent lines of blood and signs of a fight. I distinguished the marks of at least three hyenas, and followed the blood on the ground until it stopped. The distance was far. I knew that the hyenas had preyed on Hadban, or at least that's what seemed obvious." My grandmother tells this story, visibly affected. She pauses for a moment, and then continues, wiping her tearful eyes with the edge of her veil, trembling as she gestures and, with a regretful gesture, she wipes her leg. Jokingly, I asked her as I hear this story from her for the thirtieth time, without exaggeration, "What if Hadban came back, Grandma?" She responded slowly, as if pondering something distant, "Oh, by Allah, my dear, I would slaughter for him and host for him a dinner with the men."

The Overwhelming Presence of Mr. Colonel

May God be with you, my poor soul.
I spent thirty-three years in service
without gaining any benefit, without experiencing joy
or hearing a kind word
or high praise.

(1)

At first, I didn't see his face because he was standing in the front rows and I was several rows behind him, but I heard his voice and saw his head and shoulders moving as he spoke in the southern training camp. This is the largest centre, housing a large number of volunteers who are of young age, in addition to regular recruits like myself. Before the battles broke out on the front lines, every morning we would line up in long queues that I could hardly see the end of, in the square wet with rain overlooked by our barracks.

These rows did not rely on any specific order because everyone in them had low ranks or they were volunteers, most of whom came under threat or fear. It was tough days. The government confiscated many agricultural fields from the farmers, while the few who came did so out of their nationalistic fervour. I remember someone being in the second row when the sergeant threatened him with punishment, and I really don't know what he did to deserve it. He stepped forward, erect, and raised his voice as if administering a military oath: "No one punishes the Jew but the Lord." Then he followed it with a low voice and a chuckle. The rows erupted in laughter, even the leaders standing in front of us at a distance of four or five metres from the first row, their bellies shaking with laughter. Some in the back rows started to wonder, "What did the man say?"

Later on, I learned many things about Alexi, or the Jew Alexi. Much of the soldiers' talk revolved around his status and the influence he wielded in the camp. Some even swore that he worked specifically for the colonel's benefit, relaying news to him, and perhaps writing some reports or delivering them personally during his rare visits to the colonel's office, which towered on a wooden platform three meters high. It is true that his visits were infrequent, however, for a recruit, it was entirely impossible, given the circumstances, to ignore them. Many guard duties brought Alexi and me together, and a relationship formed between us that I couldn't quite understand clearly. Perhaps it was fear or hatred; I saw him like the devil who never stopped putting whispers into my ear, yet at the same time, I was impressed by him in a contention manner that depended on him. He was brave and daring. Everyone, in their respective ranks, fears mentioning the name of the colonel without attaching to it an expression of respect and esteem. Alexi used to make fun of him excessively, imitating his walk mockingly, ridiculing the way he lifted his trousers each time he came out of his office to observe us, and he raised some points that were funny enough to cast doubt into the colonel's bravery. He did many painful things. Alexi amused the officers with his sarcastic humour. The higher-ranking officers used him to ridicule the officers below them, and at the end of the day, Alexi mocked everyone. Once, when I was with him during a guard duty shift, he said to me, "As you can see, I'm not doing anything extraordinary, but you soldiers are idiots," and he hit me on my helmet.

(2)

In the summer, I met him for the first time in the trench on the front line. I remember it all, when he was stuffing his head into a fetid helmet tainted with blood and dirt he had taken from the head of a slain conscript next to him, while saying to him, "Don't be greedy, you son of a cursed woman. These things won't be useful to you any longer, and they are the right size for my head." Then he put his own old helmet on the dead soldier and said to him, "Don't worry, I won't leave your head uncovered. This will help you," and he tapped his hand twice on the helmet as if to make sure it was secure. When he saw me looking at him with dismay and fear, he said to me, as he searched the pockets of the dead soldier's trousers, "We make use of everything; you too should try and benefit yourself." That's what he said to me; I heard it quite clearly. I had just arrived with a large group of infantry soldiers from the Second Company of the Fourteenth Battalion as reinforcements for the southern front, transported in slow troop transport vehicles that caused headaches with their swaying on the dirt roads. Everyone knew they were getting close to the front before we had even arrived. Grey smoke rose from everywhere, the sounds and artillery shells never ceased to intermingle, and nothing was distinguishable. As soon as the vehicle stopped, the field officer started shouting at us, "Run, run!" while waving his hand indicating towards the trench where we were packed like ants. When I slipped into the trench with its muddy floor, it felt surreal, like everything was happening but outside of time, such that the soldiers' spit that slowly emanated from their mouths, you could follow it watching it until it fell on the ground or on someone's trousers, and similar was the case with the explosions and flying debris. The officers' shouts echoed slowly, and you could see their lips moving up and then contracting as they gave orders. The only thing that acted quickly was death.

I got used to life at the training camp far from the front. The harsh training made us sleep like the dead at night. After the morning drills, that we had done without using weapons, it would be time for rest and lunch, which we mostly spent inside our barracks – concrete rooms filled with a stench, with rusty iron doors and small windows haphazardly distributed along the wall facing the courtyard. Each room was approximately ten metres long and five or four metres wide, furnished with a set of beds covered in rough blankets, each pair of beds stacked on top of each other. We would often sleep little, only to wake up abruptly to the loud and insistent knocking on the door, even after everyone had already awakened to prepare for shooting drills.

In the evening, we would sneak quietly from our barracks to the nearby village's restaurants and bars, where Mrs. Marina would prepare chicken soup for us in her restaurant, which she and her daughter managed. Afterwards, we would have our usual evening party, drinking vodka, singing folk songs, and dancing with the military hospital nurses who were not on night duty. All of this is now over.

(3)

It is referred to in radio conversations as 'Trench No. 3,' but we, on the inside, identify it as the 'Vomit Pit'. This trench stinks intolerably, as if it's inside an animal's stomach, where all sorts of mashed-up food is dumped on you. When you enter the trench, it's like you are entering an endless maze, with long and wide corridors reinforced with wood, connected in a complex manner. In some wider corridors farther from the front line of combat, you find rooms for field command, where the radio operator and the officer who directly commands us, along with his assistants, are stationed. At the top of the trench, there are barbed wire fences you can't pass, as well as sandbags, and many bodies.

My task was to monitor the western part of the open area in front of me and listen to the conversations of the Jew Alexi, as well as to smoke the tobacco that Alexi stole from the officers' offices or from the trousers of the soldiers who fell dead. He spoke as if he were a general, with confidence and without fear of being caught by any army intelligence agents, especially when he talked about the corruption of the officers or when he mocked the colonel.

He once said to me while cleaning his rifle and without looking at me, "You're afraid of relaying my conversations to the command and getting implicated. Everyone here is afraid. And no one here knows what's happening or why we're fighting these wretches. I've never held a weapon before, and the most violent act I've ever committed in my life is encouraging my poor wife to kill a chicken. By the way, my wife cooks chicken in an irresistible way." I still remember his words clearly. I remember that he spoke passionately when he heard a rumour about an imminent ceasefire. "May the Lord curse them, all these slain go in vain, that miserable time we spent without benefit, we think of survival, then the great leaders who sleep throughout the war speak up, and when they wake up they say, 'Oh, we've slept too much while people are fighting, we must end this.' May the Lord shorten their lives." Then he lifted a metal box containing some vodka, mostly stolen, and said, "All they think about is for the man on the radio to say, "These are our great leaders achieving an amazing victory. And you, O miserable ones, here you lose your hands and heads because of the mines. What's the meaning of us fighting for several months continuously and then, without any change, they say:, 'Ceasefire!' Only the Lord knows what is happening here. Very few soldiers listen to Alexi with sadness and silence.

(4)

My dear daughter, Eva…

Why am I not receiving messages from you and from your poor mother? Read this message to her out loud and tell her that I will be back soon after we triumph over these accursed beings. All the recruits here eagerly await messages; I hope to receive one soon. I am well. Here, I have learned to use the rifle and I believe I have killed three enemy soldiers and a stray dog. Apart from that, my time is spent in surveillance and pondering over the courage of our great leader, Colonel Bodanov. I have seen him kill many enemy soldiers with a single shout;

they would collapse at the mere sound of his voice as if it were a fierce storm uprooting trees.

When we lose hope or feel afraid, we remember our great leader, Colonel Bodanov, and life surges within us, and we fight with all courage. Colonel Bodanov should not have cowardly soldiers; it does not befit his nobility and courage. Therefore, we know that those who die or flee do not deserve to be soldiers under his command. I have many stories to tell you when I return, and you will be very proud of this great leader. Here, I must cut it short due to limited time and paper. I hope you and the dog, Luke, are well, and the trees in the field too.

Private Irfa'il Alexi

May the Lord bless our great leader, Colonel Bodanov.

(5)

Despite the airstrikes coming to a cessation and the fact that direct combat had significantly reduced due to negotiations for a ceasefire, as we had expected, a mortar shell left no chance for Alexi. That was the last time I saw him, though I don't remember the exact date clearly, but the snow covered the ground. To be precise in what I say: I saw his body being carried by two men, one holding his feet and the other holding his hands, and after they waved his body in the air, they threw it into the truck that had been prepared to transport dead bodies onto a pile of other bodies, as they rotted upon each other. I was appalled when I saw them throwing his body, and felt like everything was moving very slowly. I felt sadness and dizziness, and I thought to myself: What if everything Alexi was saying was true?

Boredom and Amusement: A Way to Write a Boring Short Story

It was entertaining in the bathroom, to spray water on a dead cockroach, lying stiffly, turned on its back. Who knows what amuses people. He remembers how he used to entertain himself by throwing water-balloons at foreign workers; there were brutal invasions in those years. Entertainment began when Hameedi stole a dozen colourful balloons from the shop of Abbas the Indian, and then I stole another one. We took refuge on the roof of the mosque opposite Abbas's shop, filling the balloons with water from the mosque's washroom sinks, and gathering them in the crates Abbas would leave outside his shop. On the mosque's roof, like any artillery battalion, we waited for the perfect opportunity to attack the enemy. Whenever the street was clear of any Saudis, the throwing would begin, together with the hysterical laughter. Abbas was never directly hit except for the time he ventured out of his shop to see what curse brought the projectiles.

The white ceiling, the light fixture holding a single bulb, the electrical wiring slots, the black spot, another black spot, the recurring sound of the air conditioner fan in a steady rhythm—what is he doing now? Why am I waking up now, at 1 o' clock in the night? The smell of saliva stuck to the pillowcase, no missed call notifications, the noticing of a loose thread from his white sock. An email from Booking.com. Woke up hungry. I've always heard advice about fast food – tasty but unhealthy, tasty and unhealthy, my goodness, where's that delicious yet unhealthy food? A modest coastal town, food that's neither tasty nor healthy.

The steady recurring sound of the air conditioner fan had stopped, and the red light on the air conditioner's power button went off. The windows were covered in black adhesive, it was 1 o'clock at night, a tasteless and unhealthy dinner, and watching a film or two, then back to bed. His foot struck a trash can, which then hit the wall. The toothpaste tube was empty, so he cleaned his teeth with just the brush and water. He spat, the sound of his fingers running through his moustache hair could be heard. In the bathroom, he amused himself by spraying water on the body of a legless cockroach. He stood there observing the water flowing into the drain. He lifted the lid of the laundry basket, finding a green t-shirt and cotton underwear. Where does hunger come from? With his toes, he picked up a wipe and placed it in the trash can. The towel fell; he lifted it with his toes and then hung it on the nail in the door frame with his left hand. He didn't like leaving the bathroom door open. The hot water faucet wasn't working; once in the Sheraton Hotel in Manama, the cold water faucet wasn't working, so he asked the hotel staff to fix it. There was no one here from whom to seek the rectification of faults: no family, no friends, and no hotel staff.

He took his garment to put it on, noticing a small blue ink stain on the sleeve. The government loses a lot of ink in its employees' clothes. Radio Monte Carlo's broadcast on MW1233 was interrupted, to be replaced by World Radio on the same frequency. When the announcer asks listeners to send mail to the station's address in Cairo, he considers sending them a joke about the Christian faith. Here, the Egyptian radio broadcast is accompanied by a familiar interference. The low fuel warning light is on; to exit onto the main street, he needs to make three left turns. The red light reflects off the car parked next to him. Soft music plays on the radio – Eastern instruments with a guitar player. The sound of his palm rubbing against the steering wheel. Broken glass, an accident at 9 o'clock, an Egyptian driver in a 1999 Corolla, and a Saudi elderly man driving a 1985 Hilux. A verbal altercation, and then everything ends. 'We sell frozen chicken' is written on a large scrap of paper behind the glass. A police patrol passes slowly, the slowness of someone approaching a dangerous situation. In the restaurant, he felt a sense of relief with the lighting, like the lighting in a bar. He said to himself: "Goodness me, where's the beer? Six cans of Budweiser, ten cans, thirty-five cans, a hundred cans. I bet the world won't stand a chance against ten cans – ten cans and it'll be stumbling. And there won't be any work tomorrow." He said to the worker whose head resembled a bowling ball, "A small pizza." A black, round, hairless head, polished to perfection. It really is a bowling ball. He handed him the money, thirty-five Riyals.

The strange smell of hot plastic. In the rearview mirror, a tissue box appears behind the headrest in the back seat. No other cars can be seen on the street. What are people doing now? What do you think, you dimwit? They're sleeping, of course.

A cat stretching out, it walked along the curved path without a care. He realised he had forgotten to lock the door of the apartment. What if a thief tried to rob me? What a hapless thief he would be! By My goodness, what would he find? Do you think your respectable apartment is a gold mine? He closed the door from the inside with the key this time. If you were a fighter pilot, how exciting it would be! The freedom and the power! But would you enjoy killing people with your sophisticated aircraft? It depends on who these people are. Reflecting thoughtfully, he concluded: "And depending on the impact of this amusement on my mood, perhaps I won't like it. If I were a fighter pilot, I wouldn't have to wake up at 1 o'clock." He now remembered how his mother used to lock the pantry door so that no one would steal the wire for cleaning dishes. Back in those days, they couldn't afford to buy fireworks, so they would steal wire from their own homes, ignite one end with a lighter, and twirl it around like a whirling dervish, delighting in the sparks that would flying from it. This amusement would give me much joy. The sound of the air conditioner fan rises again. The power button on the laptop lights up with a faint green glow. Opening the downloads folder, he navigated to the "Into the Wild 2007" folder. He pulled out the plastic pizza box and placed it on the bag. He put his phone on the charger, moved closer to the ashtray, and grabbed a cold can of cola from the fridge. From the pizza, he left two full slices and the crusts of each piece he had eaten. The glow of the laptop screen reflected on his face and on the white wall, flickering on and off.

More tobacco, more cold cola, more variations in seating positions, and more reflections of lighting. He felt the cold and drowsiness at the end of the second film and said, "I must sleep." He enjoyed everything about the first movie and wished he could experience something like that solitude. He closed the laptop screen without shutting it down. He pushed away the two cola cans and the plastic bag with his foot. The grey ceiling, the single bulb in the light fixture switched off, the electrical outlets, the black spot, the other black spot, the constant rhythm of the air conditioner fan. He appreciated the coolness of the pillow and said he was happy because he didn't feel the passage of time. The light from his phone bothered him. He rolled onto his stomach and adjusted his pants with his left hand, feeling the stupor of cold creeping over everything.

In times of the past, life used to bring entertainment from every direction. Everything was aimed at bringing amusement and laughter, humble entertainment but enchanting and endless. But now, you must work hard for it. You were unaware of this hell you've embraced. You amuse yourself and laugh, yet you don't have enough money for any entertainment, no matter how basic. During the month of Ramadan, you steal tuna cans and cooked cheddar cheese for your meal. My goodness, you wretch! What pleasure is there in eating poor-quality tuna produced by a local company and cooked cheddar cheese in the women's prayer hall? I don't know, but it's certainly not the pleasure of the food itself, but rather the audacity of that meal. This stolen meal had an absolute charm that is irresistible and unforgettable. The taste of the cheddar still lingers in my mouth forever, and he moved his hand, gesturing towards a deep pleasure within.

I don't understand you, you vile creature. Everything can be a subject of entertainment, not just food. Foreign workers and innocent little children were the two preferred subjects for entertainment. We would throw stones at them or push them off their bicycles. Watching them run or fall was extremely entertaining. I bet you would enjoy that. Did you enjoy seeing your power, you son of a cursed woman? I don't know, I didn't think of it that way. We just wanted to have fun and laugh. We mocked the innocent little children, competing in making sarcastic comments about them. We tried many funny things on them: sprinkling fine dust in their eyes, pulling their pants down lightly, even lighting fire in their hair. I remember how I placed the magnifying lens on top of Ayyash's head, the boy afflicted with Down Syndrome – we didn't understand the nature of his illness back then. I moved the lens to adjust the focus of sunlight until smoke began to rise from his hateful head. I couldn't continue any further; hysterical laughter overcame me as I smelled the stench of burnt hair. O you horrible kids! We never questioned the morality of what we were doing. I suppose we wouldn't refuse to kill a crippled bird by strangling it or hitting it with shoes or any other way that brought laughter. My goodness, isn't life joyful?

I don't like the 9 o'clock sun. He greeted the manager's secretary and said to him, "I dreamt about you; you had the head of a wild donkey." He wanted to comment on the smell of tobacco but he didn't. With a blue pen, he wrote his name and the time of arrival: 7:30. He felt uneasy as he heard the sound of the pen nib moving on the page of the signature notebook. He said: "Everything has a voice, but who pays attention?" The manager's secretary replied to him, sarcastically commenting on his dream with a crude joke about the sexual abilities of a wild donkey. His hands were moving in agitation, and the papers on the desk shifted as his belly pushed against their edges. He turned over the calendar page while laughing. He said to him, "I told you, it was just the head of a wild donkey, not its whole body."

From the manager's secretary's office to his own, he passed through an infinite number of overlapping smells: the scent of cleaners, the feminine fragrance of the female employees' perfumes, the breath odour of the messenger who greeted them from afar, the emitted scent from the air conditioner, the revealing smell of falafel sandwiches, the smell of leather shoes, the dry blue ink smell, the scent of earwax, the smell of invoices, the smell of tobacco once again, until he reached the scent of his office door. He was used to drinking tea with the least amount of sugar.

A message on Facebook in the chatbox: "This message has been temporarily removed because the sender's account needs verification." More advertisements on the television screen in front of him. Engaging in the usual conversation with the department head, reminding you of some administrative memos. He noticed peeling in the colour of the hole punch. He closed the Facebook page. He said to the worker who brought him tea, "You haven't learned anything in thousands of years." The worker looked at the cup of tea and nodded in admission of his own foolishness. He said to himself, remembering something old, "What would I do with all the boring work hours without the internet? Peel potatoes, clean my nose, or sleep again," he replied, feeling the warmth of the tea in his chest. "Are you mocking me?"

"Yes, I am mocking you, dear sir. My goodness, what will you do with all the boring, miserable, trivial, and wretched hours of your life without the internet, huh?!"

"I haven't thought about this situation, but surely I'll come up with some entertainment."

"I'm happy to inform you that you'll find nothing but nonsense, sitting with clueless fools, staring at each other, sweating, repeating mythical and realistic stories every time with new details, wiping sweat from your forehead and asking about the weather, women, political news, a spat you don't know the reason for, football matches, Bashar Al-Asad, recording a video of an Egyptian dancer, a new terrorist operation, rising car prices, etc., etc., etc., of this respectable nonsense. You'll hear endless answers with different and contradictory details. And on your best nights, you'll encounter 'Mia Banat' while playing the Baloot. Do you want to spend your life in the lounge watching TV, talking, smoking, eating, playing Baloot, and going to the bathroom?"

"I don't know, I haven't thought about it before. Anyway, no matter what, we will come up with some entertainment."

"What kind of entertainment then? Look at yourself, sir, you do nothing in your delightful and enjoyable life except eat, watch films, and sleep."

"Well, as I said, no matter what, we will come up with some entertainment – entertainment without the internet."

"You really are the son of a dog."

I don't like the 12 o'clock sun, I don't like the sun at all. Who wants to eat tasteless and unhealthy food at noon?

When he left work, the sun was in the sky and the humidity was everywhere. He felt the heaviness of the damp air, the damp and musty air. Why stay in the office? What about a lunch that's neither tasty nor healthy, but he also wanted to sleep. "Without sleep, I'd hang himself."

The key turned easily in the apartment door lock. He noticed a loose red thread from the scarf, and the repetitive sound of the air conditioner fan resumed its steady rhythm. The red light on the air conditioner's power button lit up.

He resisted the deep temptation to withdraw from work before the designated end time. The sound of the pen moving across the green signature notebook paper passed in his ears. The light from his phone reflected on his face, and he felt the air from the air conditioner enveloping him. What would he do if he woke up. If he could afford to sleep for a whole week, he would not hesitate. The white ceiling, he pondered over his existence without continuous hours of watching YouTube, without trivial and important messages on his phone, without Twitter, Facebook, SoundCloud, without downloading more movies, he tapped his cigarette on the ashtray, and no internet connection.

The person sleeping said slowly, "Existence will become boring, and you will be burdened with the idea of getting rid of meaningless gigabytes of trivialities." The white ceiling disappearing, he admired the texture of the cotton cover. Tedious yet light, its monotony fills us with joy. My goodness, where is this boring non-burdensome existence, you true son of a dog.

The white ceiling, the light fixture holding a single bulb, the electrical sockets, the black spot, the other black spot, the steady recurring sound of the air conditioner fan, what is he doing now? Why did he wake up now, at 9 pm? He felt a slight twist in his neck, the filled bladder bothered him. The light from the mobile phone screen was bright, 9:12 pm. Three messages on WhatsApp. In the mirror above the ceramic sink, he saw a scrawny face, took a sip of water from the tap, and washed his face. He thought about the gluey slime stuck inside the water channel.

In the bathroom, he didn't find a dead cockroach. His left foot slipped and hit the toilet, he lifted his left foot and pressed it with his hand. He washed his hands with water but was too lazy to clean his teeth. He turned on the TV – a presenter speaking fast. He lit a cigarette – it was the last one in the packet. No one hungry was coming. He threw the cigarette packet in front of him. He wiped the screen of his mobile phone with his right thumb. He pressed on his left foot to ease the pain. On TV, there was a Serie A match – he didn't know if it was being broadcast live or recorded. He adjusted his seating position. He made a cup of tea with little sugar, but he couldn't find the mint. An Egyptian presenter was overwhelming him with sleepiness.

A new packet of cigarettes – he lit another one. He thought how the flavour of the tobacco would be great with a good cup of tea. He was annoyed by the remote control's weak response, so he smacked it on the floor. The battery cover slipped off. He despaired over the limited number of channels, muted the TV on a programme from the Nineties where someone spoke in a dubbed language about the Olympic Games.

The power button on the laptop glowed with a faint green light. He wiped the middle of the laptop screen with his right thumb. At the top of the browser, the red YouTube logo was clear – the homepage. An endless number of other video recommendations. He searched for a song by his favourite singer,

Aseel Hameem. After the first minute, he noticed a video on the left side of the page of Aamaal Maher performing a song by Muhammad Abdu. He enjoyed the clarity of the rhythm. He wished he were in Bahrain now, listening to this song. He said to himself: "I've heard stupid and annoying songs in the bars I've been to. I want a table in the dark part of the bar, a good internet connection, and smoke, more beer, and when I get hungry, I want a huge never-ending piece of steak, with grilled potatoes." He felt hungry and got up to prepare himself a cheese spread sandwich, but he couldn't find any bread. He cursed and took the cheese cup to eat it with a spoon. He turned on the air conditioner and wanted to watch something short and entertaining on YouTube. But what's entertaining, you real son of a dog? He watched several clips of comedy shows that weren't funny but helped pass the time. When you eat cheese spread with a spoon, its taste is strong.

He watched a strange video clip of a man talking to the devil, then a video clip of two boys fighting in a neighbourhood in Jeddah. A warning message on the mobile screen about data usage. He was slightly displeased by the taste of the cheese spread. He thought about another cup of tea. In the freezer compartment, he found a Reese's chocolate wrapped in foil, and he felt like he had done a wise thing when he left it the first time. He smiled, and he pondered over the mistake of those who eat chocolate to satisfy their hunger, and he began eating it with enjoyment. He called his childhood friend whom he hadn't spoken to in a while, wanting to ask him about the chance of spending the weekend in Bahrain, but he didn't answer. He cursed his childhood friend and all those who work in the Eastern Province. He stretched out and brought the laptop closer to him. He opened the folder of films – countless films – from Hollywood blockbusters to independent European films. He thought about watching a film about World War II or rewatching his beloved film Mary and Max, but he reconsidered and started watching the Peaky Blinders series after remembering the enthusiastic recommendation he read about it. Without dinner this time, he watched three consecutive episodes from the first season. The laptop screen's light reflected on his face and on the white wall, flickering on and off. More tobacco, more cold cola, more different sitting positions, and more reflections of light. At that moment, he felt a sense of relief from everything, a powerful wave of tranquillity engulfing him. He stood up to urinate, wondering in the bathroom how this immersion in watching could put him this great mood. It was like someone who understood the meaning of his existence, despite not grasping anything clearly. He didn't feel hungry, not even a hint of hunger. He wanted to continue watching endlessly. More watching, my goodness.

He watched the fourth episode, pressing his thumb and forefinger on his eyes, then the fifth episode as well. Time was getting late. He said to himself: "I'll finish watching the sixth episode and then sleep." He drank more cola, annoyed by his need to urinate again. In the bathroom, while urinating standing up, he said to himself: "Do you know, you son of a dog, that you're such a fool? A fool of the highest degree. You think only about trivialities that resemble you. You're empty except for the residue in your intestines."

"What do you want me to do? That's the situation anyway. What do you do?"

"Go out and kill someone, wouldn't that entertain you?"

"No, I want to sleep now."

When he left the bathroom, he felt a headache and pain in his eyes. With all his heart, he wanted to sleep forever, prostrating himself as he thought about one last trip to Bahrain before entering this eternal sleep. The grey ceiling, the light socket holding the single bulb switched off, the electrical outlets, the black spot, the other black spot, the sound of the air conditioning fan repeating at a steady rhythm.

Nightmares of a Journalist Who Wants to Write a Short Story on the Battle of the Chinese Farm

On the night when he left the window of the room open, it was on that night when the summer air moved the curtain, and on that night specifically, he had a strange dream, and the strangeness was not in the content of the dream, no… no. The peculiarity, however, is that the dream causes him depression despite not remembering it clearly when he wakes up. It was on that night that he dreamt of himself sitting inside a trench on the frontline east of the canal after crossing the Bar Lev Line. He was dressed in a modest military uniform and shouldered an old rifle. Sitting beside him was a recruit whose body was not clearly defined. The recruit asked many questions and smoked, listening to a small wooden radio broadcasting Israeli deception.

The recruit said, "You too will die, but not in your bed, rather in the Battles of the Chinese Farm." He smoked a whole cigarette in silence, then, pointing to his shoulder, he said, "An officer from the paratrooper battalion will strike you with his fire. Perhaps his name is Saul," mimicking the sound of gunfire.

He said to him, incredulously, "It doesn't matter."

The recruit pulled out a photograph from his wallet showing a shy girl standing in an orange field, "This is my beloved daughter. You can marry her if you want," he chuckled.

He quietly passed it to him.

The recruit said, "I don't want war, but what do we do when these Americans are occupying our land?"

He replied, "They are not Americans."

The recruit said angrily, "It doesn't matter, I'm not afraid of them," and he extended his hand, raising four fingers, "We have crushed three armoured brigades and an infantry division. We've downed all their aircraft." He fell silent, and after a moment he said, "If things had carried on in this way, we would have won, my brother." Then he took a long silence.

He asked him, "Do you want to eat?"

The recruit replied, "No. I need to urinate," then added irritably, "You're dreaming now while I'm here fighting the Americans, my brother."

When I wake up at around seven or eight from a disturbing dream – I'm not exactly sure what was disturbing about it – I feel a sense of gloom, not because it was a disturbing dream, but because I feel a responsibility towards something I can't quite understand. Thoughts swirl in my mind as I sit on the edge of the bed trying to go back to sleep. My bladder was bothering me, so I got up to urinate. I thought to myself that the bladder is a good alarm clock. My father was sitting on the couch, focused on watching television, commenting about the economic situation.

From the kitchen came the sound of the electric grinder.

When I returned to my bed, I reached for the cigarette packet; I wanted to smoke one cigarette and then go back to completing my sleep, but the lighter didn't work. I stood up and went to the gas stove in the kitchen; the blue flame of the stove was comforting. I stood there for a while, watching it quietly as I smoked. My mother said I was annoying her with this smoke, then asked me to wash my face, prepare for dinner, and to go on the balcony if I wanted to smoke. My father sonorously joined us from his place, telling my mother, "Your son does nothing in his life except sleep." I turned off the stove and returned to bed.

The time on my mobile phone screen approached 8 o'clock. I couldn't find an ashtray nearby, so I extinguished the cigarette on the edge of the wooden bed frame and tossed the butt behind the nightstand. I stretched out and closed my eyes, anxious about a dream I don't clearly recall but remember vaguely. I hoped to myself not to have any dreams. Time, in sleep, passes without awareness, or at least on a meaningless black screen.

He had a strange dream on a cold, misty night inside a trench on the frontline along the Bar Lev Line, where he saw himself wearing a military uniform, sitting on the ground, and beside him was President Anwar Sadat, looking at a field map that General Saad el-Din el-Shazly had spread out in front of him. The President was wearing an elegant suit, with a military jacket on his head to shield him from the heavy rain. General Saad el-Shazly was very authoritative, speaking loudly so that the President could hear him; the intermittent sound of the artillery was deafening to the ears. General el-Shazly pointed on the map while speaking angrily, "You requested support for the attack, but now look what happened!" President Anwar Sadat responded, surprised by el-Shazly's audacity, "I gave you an order, and you must execute it, because you don't understand politics. We do not want to defeat the Israelis; we want a strong position on the ground so that when we negotiate with them, we negotiate from a position of strength, sir!"

El-Shazly listened, speaking repeatedly about mobilising some brigades, but then Sadat abruptly pulled the map, stained with mud, and said, "No one is withdrawing, not a single rifle, or I'll throw you in prison." Everything was clear in the dream as if it were an image on the television: SAM missiles pursuing planes in the dark sky, dazzling artillery lights, armoured personnel carriers chasing and crushing soldiers. However, later, when he wakes up, he will forget, and the foggy image of Sadat will remain unclear, not remembering if he spoke about victory, or something about artillery, officer accountability, or something along these lines. But regardless, when he wakes up and smokes his first cigarette, he will feel depressed.

The only dream that haunted the officer who served in the Haim Brigade in the Israeli Occupation Forces: was the dream of the officer who may have been named Saul, who used to stutter in his childhood and was the target of mockery by his colleagues at school for the lack of coordination in his eye movement due to weakness in his left eye muscles; who was harassed by his neighbour's daughter – nine years his senior - in his adolescence; who stole from the money his mother had hidden in her clothes cabinet; who nearly drowned when he started swimming lessons which he later abandoned; who learned to smoke at an early age while going out with his friends, loitering in the nearby streets; who had a fear-filled conversation with his father on the issue of migrating to America; and who didn't know that his uncle was killed at the end of Rue de Rivoli in a skirmish near the Place de la Concorde after joining the French Resistance against the Nazis; who didn't complete his studies at the Law School; the one for whom a promotional photo was taken, standing on top of an armoured vehicle in camouflage attire with an unshaven chin, appearing next to him on the top of the vehicle was a small red flag; who, if he hadn't been killed in the Battle of the Chinese Farm, would now be a father of two children and attending a mental health clinic on Indiana Avenue; who met General Ariel Sharon and greeted him in the areas adjacent to the Abu Tartour Road east of the Canal; and who was killed by an anti-tank missile in the Battle of the Chinese Farm, fired by Staff Sergeant Muhammad Muhammad Mamoun. This officer had a recurring dream that persisted every night after the 1967 war. He saw himself holding a thick stick, pushing forward his rolling head in front of him in endless yellow sand dunes.

I received a call from my friend, who typically starts our conversations with "Where are you, my lad?" After he asked me to come out, I informed him that I would catch up with him shortly. At around 10 o'clock, I had entered the coffee shop and saw him gesturing with his long arm and calling out loudly. I shook his hand without him getting up from his place. As I sat down and he turned his head towards me and asked me, with hookah smoke billowing from his mouth, if I had any hashish. I replied, laughing, "I don't have anything."

He was as he always was, impulsive and careless, yet kind. Since our childhood, he had shared with me everything good he acquired, as well as his problems. I wanted to mention the topic of dreams with him, but I didn't say anything to avoid making it seem forced. He said to me, "Look," taking a drag from the hookah hose, "what happened with the crazy mother-in-law this time?" and then he started telling me about his mother-in-law, whose daughter he had divorced in less than a year after marriage. I placed the cigarette packet and lighter on the table, and I began to light my cigarette from the coals on top of the hookah, listening to him and occasionally offering brief supportive comments. Sounds emanated from everywhere: mouths, hookahs, televisions, mobile phones, the refrigerator compressor, and the sound of water boiling in the kettle, as well as the cars outside. While he was still talking about his issue with his mother-in-law, he ordered some koshary tea. Then he started laughing and said that he envied me for not getting involved in this marriage business. He asked me, "Have you completed the procedures for issuing medical insurance for your father?" and asked the coffee shop worker to change the charcoal on the hookah. I lit another cigarette from the charcoal before he changed it. I told him I was waiting for a medical report to be issued. He turned to me with his full body as if remembering something significant and asked me, while gesturing with the hookah hose, to accompany him to Ismailiyyah. He said to me, "To offer condolences to an old friend whose father passed away."

He tried to jog my memory, saying that I had met him once or twice. I remembered him when he told me that he was the one with us when our car broke down on the 6th of October

Bridge. I told him that I might not be able to go; in truth, I was hesitant to travel such a distance for someone I had only met once, perhaps he might not even remember me. He said we wouldn't be late. I lit another cigarette with my lighter and told him I would think about it. I asked for another cup of tea, koshary tea. He was playing a combat game or something like that on his mobile phone and gestured for me to look at the television; I saw Yasmin Sabri on the screen in a recorded interview with Esaad Younis; she looked beautiful and charming. He enthusiastically commented, "This the Yasmin – the goddess of beauty according to the ancient Egyptians," and laughed. Then he cursed and said he lost some points because of her. I told him, "It's okay," and he looked at me disgustedly as he took the coal off the hookah with the apartment key. He remained silent and resumed his game. He asked for another hookah head and placed his mobile phone on the table. He asked me about the work news in the newspaper, and I told him everything is as it was. The coffee shop worker changed the hookah head and placed a new charcoal. I lit a cigarette from the hookah coal and told him, "I'm working on writing a short story about the October War. I've watched many testimonies of Egyptian officers and officers of the occupying forces on recorded films, speeches by Sadat in parliament, and that I've read Arabic and translated works about the war, including what Sadat and other military leaders had written about it. I recorded observations on more than forty pages about everything, including character patterns, weapons used, the numbers of casualties and prisoners, daily developments on the front lines. I also documented drawings and diagrams illustrating the locations and movements of military sectors. This work is exhausting; artistic work is not easy because you have to know everything as if you have seen it yourself and participated in it. Then after this fatigue, you use less than a third of this knowledge." He replied consolingly and said that the stories I write are good. He asked me to send him the text by email. I told him that I had only written one sentence, lit another cigarette, and read him the only sentence I had written: **In fact, the matter involved a funny misconception, as the Chinese Farm, named after the battle, was actually a Japanese farm.**

He seemed somewhat enthusiastic as he listened. He said it wasn't funny, but rather an intriguing start, that's what he said. I talked to him about the story's subject and told him that the essence of the story wasn't about the war but about the political impact on military action in the October War. I told him that Sadat compelled the military leadership to execute failed orders, to the extent that the Israelis besieged the Third Field Army because of his decisions. I told him that we lost the war, and I cursed Sadat.

He laughed and said that these mistakes happen, and the important thing is that Sinai was liberated. I began to be annoyed by the density of the smoke in the coffee shop, and said that they are not mistakes but rather part of the context, and like a wise Greek philosopher who discovered the secret of existence but in a caricatured manner, I said that there is nothing arbitrary; everything is subject to a context, even the embers of your hookah. He laughed and didn't comment. I said to him, "Perhaps the matter will evolve, and I'll write a novel about the political impact not only on military action but on everything: religion, language, economy, ethics, humanities, the street in front of your house. And I could start with the October War."

I felt a mysterious happiness as I spoke about my work. He said it would be a good novel, then asked me with interest why I don't collect the stories I've written and publish a story collection, "I'm not interested at the moment," I replied. He mentioned that he once read that the American University in Kuwait had placed a $20,000 prize, and he encouraged me to publish my collection and participate. Then he said that if I were to win this prize, we could start any project from then on. I remained silent. I lit a cigarette and told him that something strange had happened to me while preparing to write this story, and to justify the oddity, I told him that I had written many stories and this had never happened to me before. Then I told him about the unsettling, unclear nightmares that had been haunting me since I started gathering material for the story. He laughed, and with the laughter came dense smoke. "Perhaps these nightmares are a result of political influence," he said, asking me about the nightmares. I told him they were disturbing nightmares that I couldn't recall clearly, but they were all about the October War. I think I saw el-Shazly fighting himself, tanks running over recruits, cold nights in Al-Matariyyah, the crying of women. I don't know many things that cause disturbance. Oh, once I saw three occupation soldiers on the balcony looking at me through the glass in its door. They didn't attack me, but every time I hid, I felt like they were still watching me.

I understood from the dream that they wanted to kill me. That was the clearest nightmare I had. He told me, "This was due to overdosing on reading about the war," and that I had exhausted myself. I told him that perhaps I should just stick with that sentence which I had written and forget about this nightmare story. He laughed and said that the important thing is to publish your story collection. I fell silent, lit a cigarette, and ordered another cup of koshary tea.

My mother lived a marginal part of her childhood in an underground shelter. It was a primitive shelter that my grandfather had dug with the help of his brother in the backyard of their home – an old traditional house in Ain Shams. Using basic tools, they dug a trench. Then they made for it a roof from palm tree branches and palm leaves, wooden beams, and covered it with soil. This was during the 1967 war when the sky was a playground for Israeli warplanes. In the evenings, they would turn off all the lights and prepare for the possible descent into the shelter. As a young child, my mother hated the Jews, believing that there was nothing in the world except Egypt and the Jews, and that when this conflict ended, the Day of Judgement would come and the world would end. As she grew older, she began to resent the occupiers and realised that history was broader than this conflict. The shelter became a place where her grandchildren played until it collapsed on its own, perhaps tired of waiting for the war to end without any result, or perhaps angry about the peace treaties.

Reflections on the Absence of Joys

The abnormality of staying in the radiant city with its commercial billboards

Crowded, crowded and suffocating. Shoulder to shoulder, the breath of the man who ate a plate of beans and raw onions for breakfast in your face, a sagging stomach for a small man in a sweaty shirt sticking to your back, and a tired-looking black man distinguished by a stiff moustache, thick smoke emanating, and the smell of burning wild animal intestines. A broken elevator packed with a woman – suffering from cat allergies, her driver, and her screaming son, along with four large travel bags, and a strong-built, indifferent Ethiopian maid. The woman cried and sprawled despondently on the elevator floor. She slouched in the elevator, for which, on the floor far above, on the ninety-seventh floor, thirteen Bangladeshi workers of the cleaning company waited, the company for which the man who had eaten a plate of beans and raw onions, whose mouth was near your nose, worked.

Crowded, crowded and strange. Endless notice panels, in the kitchen with the smell of burning animal intestines, in the bedroom, panels in the pool too, mostly notices for maintenance of water pipes, and in the women's prayer room too. In the oil change pit, I saw a panel, commercial panels crowded on top of each other like a mound of bison skulls, starting from the Parisian brand boutiques to the local shops in the alleys run by workers with expired residency permits. The restaurant that accommodates only four people is crowded with hundreds of customers, selling beef slices seasoned with spices made by a Nigerian woman complaining of back pains. The black man cutting beef in the restaurant now wipes his sweat and responds to a call from a female Ethiopian worker working for a woman stuck in an elevator; the iron smells of damp, mouldy cheese, and the oversized rats, sometimes weighing a kilogramme, acting as if they were wildcats, multiplying in cargo shipments coming from Eastern Europe, Iran, and India, in the port, on the beach, in large waste containers, and in the crevices of popular houses. They breed in the kitchen that smells of burning animal intestines, in the bedroom, in the storage rooms of famous shops whose names we cannot mention.

Crowded, crowded and distressing. A stream of cars moving unsystematically; cars barely appearing before disappearing into side streets like fleeing cockroaches; cars drop from above and emerge from under manhole covers; and from windows too do cars emerge. The asphalt road is bad, and my small car can't bear all of that. On the road, as you try to catch up with your work appointment, there are piles of silent concrete barriers, silent and eternal. You might encounter on your way, as you try to catch up with your work appointment, a wardrobe – a wooden wardrobe, and playing with its doors are the air currents created by the passing cars trying to avoid it. You might encounter a tired-looking black man distinguished by a firm moustache, the body of a girl with her abdomen exposed drowned in the floods that swept through the city, black holes but they are holes in the ground, wild animals that were actually humans, and you might encounter other things but I don't know what they are. And, of course, you will come across water whose nature you do not notice, flowing out of the building you are passing by now while you are busy searching for a buffet you remember nearby. The damp human waste overflows from the toilet bowl like sea slugs, dark and heavy. After the overflowing water reached the living room, and reached the outer door of the apartment, which does not exceed an area of 30 square meters, and is inhabited by a family of two parents and seven boys and a girl, and another girl infected with leprosy but symptoms have not appeared on her yet, the woman who wanted to go out but stood on the couch to take cover from the overflowing water and the dark slugs said, "May God curse your filth!" She felt nauseous and helpless and said to someone who was sleeping: "Get up! Look at what's happening!" In the evening when she cried while in the bathroom trying to unclog the drain, her bound throbbing head hurting her, a mosquito – which was really a crow, landed on her earlobe. She heard her son's voice calling out to her in fear because his nose was bleeding black, thick blood. She said, "God curse me for leaving you," and she cursed herself with a very ugly curse that we do not want to mention. A person knocked on the door of the apartment, which does not exceed an area of 30 square meters, who was sent by another person, when she answered him from behind the door with a stammer, he said to her that they owe the drainage maintenance fee, and they owe the rent. The house phone rang, and it was another man calling for her, not the one who was sleeping. The girl who is not afflicted with leprosy tells her that her apron is torn. She must also prepare the utensils, clean the baby who is now crying, and perform the Maghrib ritual prayer whose time has passed.

Crowded, crowded and I don't know what to say. The man working in the real estate office, which opens onto a street whose name we don't want to mention, said to the man sitting in front of him, perplexed, "Don't bother us, may God help you." The man sitting confused felt bitterness and didn't know what to do. He got into his car, which he bought from an Egyptian working in a private clinic, whom he had known for years. Before leaving for good in a few weeks, he sold it to him for 8,000. The Egyptian, working as a doctor in a private clinic, knew a pharmacist who had been struck with a machete on his shoulder after attempting to resist a 40 year-old man who raided the pharmacy. He stood in front of him, where the pharmacist was sitting, playing with his mobile phone and feeling bored. The 40 year-old man, who was confused at that hour, said, "Take out the money, all of it." He struck the glass of the display table with his machete. He had inherited this machete from his father, who used it to break the bones of sacrificial animals on Eid morning, nearly thirty years ago. The pharmacist felt death approaching. The Bangladeshi who worked with him at the pharmacy called the police. The report came to a soldier who parked his patrol car next to the 'Buffet of Happiness,' located on a side street run by an Indian who contemplated suicide after the government confiscated the agricultural land he had earned from working in this buffet. The soldier thought to himself, "Keep us distracted," and precisely at that moment, said the woman living in an apartment no larger than 30 square meters, sitting in the kitchen with her back against the refrigerator door, "Where do we get money from?" A dark-skinned man passed by the building in the street, calling out to another man in the distance. The woman, leaning against the refrigerator door and annoyed by the foul smell of the dirty pots, thought the voice came from one of the neighbours. As for the girl who had leprosy but hadn't shown symptoms yet, she was afraid of the confines of the carehome on a hard bed, feeling humiliated and exposed.

Crowded, crowded and distressing. The Nigerian woman, who complains of back pains and prepares spices to season beef, is feeling angry, and agitated like an epileptic woman, because her uncle called her and spoke to her in a stern tone while he sat with four of his relatives, informing her that their son had been kidnapped. The man whose wife said to him, "Get up! Look at what's happening!" was captured by surveillance cameras as he stormed into the pharmacy with a machete. He hadn't hidden the machete; pushed the door that said: "Convey Blessings to Muhammad," stood there; smashed the glass of the display table; and ordered the pharmacist to hand over the money, saying, "Listen! I'm not a thief, I just want three thousand. If Allah blesses me with a profit, I'll repay you. Damn you."

During the day, the woman who worked at a private school near the pharmacy waited for the driver, cried, then decided to continue walking on her way, as she didn't have the three thousand, as her wages were delayed.

Crowded, crowded and sticky. As you walk, you might superficially ponder about things that could bring you money, perhaps even imagining the ease of starting a small business. The humidity and high temperature weigh heavily on you, the heavy air passes hotly through the crevices of your nose, sweat appears dry on your white clothes, and you feel the breath of the man who had breakfast with a plate of beans, eggs, and raw onions, his breaths tickling your neck as if they were insect-like, close and warm, and the sound of his breathing scratching at the membrane of your brain, the disturbing noises reaching a crescendo, the sweat is profuse, and the Yemeni man rubs his head with a dirty towel soaked in sweat. You sit in the back seat of the car near the door, with an Afghani man stuck next to you, to whom is stuck another Afghani man, and the fourth man among you, an Egyptian, who doesn't hear too well and doesn't seem to mind this suffocating atmosphere. If you took a look outside the window, you would see shiny billboards running, and a sewage tanker standing, its rear hose extending into a manhole, a manhole teeming with rats and mice that behave as if they were wildcats. The man sitting in the driver's seat of the sewage tanker doesn't feel nauseous and wishes he could finish early to eat a plate of lentils from a Yemeni vendor who wipes his head with a towel soaked in sweat. Your breath diminishes, and the oppressive heat of the air is oppressive, affecting your mood, and the headache pounds your forehead like nails. You won't find any work. You tell yourself, feeling lonely, realising that staying in these places requires money, selling, buying, sleeping, eating, friendship, hypocrisy, sitting in the car, renting an apartment, unclogging drains, respect, and oh, returning home, washing the dry yellow sweat off your clothes, and everything else you haven't thought of, everything requires money.

Your head collides with the Afghan's head and the window glass. The Egyptian man, who doesn't hear too well, says to the driver, "Take it easy, sir." Do you feel annoyed? The blow from the Afghan's head hurts you, I tell you the truth: if you don't have money now, your pain means nothing but more despair. You rub your forehead with your hand, trying to warn your head so it doesn't ache without your consent. You see billboards that keep running before your eyes in eternal repetition, over-shadowing everything you might see.

On those bonds that I have forgotten, well:

The sun was clear and vibrant, its summery rays foretelling a warm winter's day. It was one of those varied January days deserving of an indescribable euphoria, a happiness derived from your distant days, your childhood days when you sat on the kitchen table watching your mother clean a tilapia fish, gutting it, and scaling it. The sunlight escaping through the wide window above the sink evoked a sense of intimacy towards your mother. You play from your place on the table with the salt and black pepper shakers, moving them as if they were two cars. Your mother looks at you spontaneously, and she laughs, holding out the severed fish tail in your face to frighten you cheerfully, while the sound of the television comes to you in a low tone, appropriate to the sound of a television on the first day of the week. The dark wooden colors covering the kitchen floor and the smell of orange peels that the mother was roasting on the stove, all created a comforting aura around this memory that you recall now on a warm January day.

On the beach outside the city, in an uninhabited place, the white foam of the waves surging with force, crashing against the stone barrier cubes, then rising high. The sea waves, the cold air that causes the eyes to shed tears, the seagulls competing for a headless fish, soaring and diving. The heavy scent of the sea, a mysterious fear seized him of the power of the waves and the vastness of the sea. The imported palm tree standing with its tall trunk. He wished he had a cigar with him now.

He sat on the white wooden chair, while on the other white chair sat a beautiful girl, with an old grandmother from Sana'a, who always says "Bismillah" before doing anything. She watched the sea, not knowing why she remembered the afternoon sun in the living room, the large windows close to the ground, and the embroidered chiffon curtains. The sounds of children playing around the pool, the feeling of the calm air emanating from the ceiling vents, relaxing on the couch and reading a novel written by Balzac in English, and piano lessons with Miss Safaa in the living room, the note of 'doh' at the end of the Persian musical mode ringing in her ears. This was her second cigar.

She looked at his eyes, and he too gazed silently at the sea. Slowly, he said to her, "Everything has happened contrary to what I wanted, and against my nature." He didn't look at her. He glanced sadly at the anklets on her legs, longing to hold her hand, but he feared that with this sudden impulse he might appear weak or clumsy. She said, "I don't want to talk about anything," as the sound of the waves crashing against the stone barrier grew stronger and sharper. He reached for her cigarette packet, she didn't look, and extended the lighter to him. He stood up and took two or three steps. "If only I could throw myself into the sea right now." He felt ashamed of himself for not having the strength to confront these matters.

He smoked and returned to sit, not looking at her eyes. He wished he could cry now and end all this anxiety; he couldn't bear this burden. He said to her despairingly, as he looked at the anklets, his body almost leaning towards the ground, "Can you forget what happened?" The words came out heavily, it was as if they had been ripped from his soul, the sound of the waves crashing against the rocky barrier.

She said, while feeling some affection towards him and wishing she could forget and everything could return to how it was, "Nothing critical has happened." And she fell silent. In her own mind, a bleak outlook on existence appeared, not clear but signifying the notion of the limited joys in this existence. When your life is going truly well, that's the perfect time for the axe to fall and split you in half. After all, humans aren't trees to withstand a sharp, iron blow of an axe. When you feel the strength and happiness of ownership enveloping your soul and see the effectiveness of money with your very own eyes, rare epidemics might strike you, or your family might be torn apart, or your skin might peel off, or a Boeing plane might crash onto you as you walk without a helmet. Then she realised that all of this could happen to her without having any power, even when she feels insignificant and worthless. That's how she imagined it. He said to her, seeing the sunlight reflecting off her anklet, "We can start everything anew if these times pass, please. Let's live in America this time. I'll claim my share, then we will leave. We'll have a good life." She wanted to say that this goes against her nature, but she remained silent. Then she said, looking at the sea with sorrow, "You don't understand," and she repeated what she said because when she uttered "… understand," it coincided with the sound of the waves crashing against the rocky barrier, "You have never understood me." He took hold of her hand, intending to kiss the back of it, but in that moment, he was confused and unable to articulate a coherent thought, so he raised her hand towards his chest and wept. I remember that when he was young, he wanted to do something spectacular, something that would make him proud until the last day of his life with that power. Everyone would ask, "Who is it that did this?" Oh, what a mischievous boy he was, and he thought that at that moment he would hide his smile because no one else would know who did it. And it didn't occur to his mind anything more foolish or trivial than destroying the board with ink when all the students began to leave for recess after the third period. He pretended to write down a lesson in his maths notebook, making his delay in the class seem natural, just a part of a normal school day. And after some time had passed and he was sure that everyone had gone out for recess, he broke a pen, a liquid blue ink pen, but he struggled to break another red one. He used his teeth to break the pen's tip and used the chair's leg. The blue ink looked dark, almost black, and then he started drawing lines vertically and horizontally on the board until it became difficult to write on it for the teacher in the next class. When recess concluded and the rest of the students returned, the teacher entered, and another heavy maths class began. Nothing happened because the lines on the board were ineffective. In contrast, the ink stains on his hands and next to his mouth were powerful and visible stains, effective spots. As for now, he is crying and trying to regain his composure so that he doesn't lose control and does not against his intention. She withdrew her hand, and he felt ashamed of his own broken self. He composed himself and said to her in a desperate manner, as if reciting a poem, "Despite everything you see, you didn't see my torn soul, my empty soul. Without you, I am miserable and I find no meaning in all this nonsense." He closed his eyes and said, "Please." She too was sad, despite everything. She looked out at the horizon where seagulls soared, the sunlight, the cold air. She said, "I didn't do anything." She wanted to say, "You ruin our joys," but she didn't. What's the point? She lit another cigarette. Angry, thinking that he deserved the pain, and that her connection with him was futile, and everything else was useless. He looked at the anklet on her leg and said, "My heart is breaking and I will never be happy, and I am a human after all. Please."

The impact of hunger on the mind of a young man lurking under the coffee shop table and speaking:

"From this damp cellar, from this crumbling cellar with its suffocating smell and stale air. From this rented cellar filled with strange types of dead insects, and from this cellar whose walls have peeled off like the shedding skin of a reptile, from this charred cellar that was previously used to store onion bags. From this mouldy and sick cellar, yes, sick, from this lavatory-like cellar, with its dim lighting and low ceiling, with just one lamp, a lamp that swung from above. A few old papers, with dirty old clothes, and unable to provide sufficient food, and this is bad. After being fired from my job at the public library because they discovered that I was sleeping there after work. From this cellar, after swallowing some food and having in my stomach a mixture of warm milk, mashed potatoes, and water, which is enough to stimulate the brain for tonight. From this cellar, I want to write to you about happiness. Don't laugh. I hope you show me some respect. Anyway, I won't tell you who I am, so none of you can exploit anything against me. Therefore, your respect won't matter. And that's clear. In fact, I don't know what happiness is, and that's disappointing. But also, I'm not interested in knowing what happiness is, and I don't care if it's just a physiological process of hormones and neurotransmitters and those incomprehensible things, or an internal feeling emanating from the soul or from anywhere else. The essence of the matter regarding happiness, and this will make what I say fundamentally important in every future discussion about happiness, even after decades, and I may be exaggerating, but I honestly believe that I am a great person, not in terms of greatness in my personality as you can see, but in this essence of what I express and those papers that I write. Anyway, I don't want to digress into trivial matters. I say that the essence of the matter regarding happiness is my discovery – and it is a discovery not favoured by anyone, which came after my being expelled from work and not finding a place to sleep, and after long sessions in the bathroom, you know those great ideas that come while ejecting what the stomach doesn't want from the mixture of warm milk, mashed potatoes, and tomato skins floating in the stomach above the milk. Anyway, that's not important – the inevitable connection between happiness and willpower is achievement. Don't rush and mock the wording of the text. As you can see, I work within tight constraints, and if I were in a better position than this, I would be a respected man, and everyone would say, "What a genius!" Yet they find themselves faced with the same wording which they mock. Happiness, as I tell you, is inherently linked to willpower achievement, which means I understand how happiness occurs, although I don't know its nature. Well, if you accept this great addition from me, which will change the course of social sciences, I will further expand my investigation of this matter, but such research requires a sharp mind, and even a mind that is sharp, needs food to provide it with energy. I hope none of you would think that I am asking for food in exchange for what I say. Please don't think in this provocative way. Anyway, we won't expand on topics that are not important. Well, when a person wants something – no matter how big or small, evil or good – they do what fulfils that desire, but it is unfortunate that with this consumerism, more desires accumulate than the capacity of this world. I am not one of those who are driven by their desires, and I have chosen or been forced due to these circumstances you see to defer all desires that arise in my mind without knowing their source except for those desires that I cannot postpone, like eating, sleeping, going to the bathroom, and contemplating, of course. Well, when a person finds that a desire comes to their mind from a source he does not know – not all human desires are rational, so please don't think in this superficial way – they begin to take actions that bring them closer to fulfilling that desire. If the desire is fulfilled, the person feels a certain level of happiness, a happiness that has a certain level of intensity in the person's feeling and its temporal duration, depending on the person's attachment to that desire. If the desire is not fulfilled, the person feels a certain level of sadness. Well, someone who thinks in the contrary manner might say: Why do we feel sad when someone we love dies? I pondered on this, after drinking a glass of milk and swallowing some mashed potatoes that I didn't quite enjoy the taste of. We grieve because we want them to stay, and with their death, achieving this desire becomes impossible. Our realisation of this impossibility is what leads us to cry and accumulates sorrow in our hearts. However, as I hear the mice scratching behind the peeling wooden walls, I say to you, "I need some clarification on certain matters, so that none of you think that what I've said has no value." Human desires are not that simple; I mean, they are complex and intricate. When a nation is under foreign occupation, a desire for liberation of the homeland emerges among the common people, and this liberationist desire conflicts with the occupier's desire for staying and domination. Since the nature of our existence does not allow for the realisation of two conflicting desires in the same time and place, a conflict between the two parties will occur to fulfil the will of the stronger of the two. And when the will of the occupied people is not fulfilled, a general sense of sadness spreads at various levels. It's not pure sadness because humans are complex beings anyway, and the occupied people may even feel happiness when their will is realised in other aspects, at least when their national football team wins, and so on.

It seems like I might have started to ramble incoherently, do you understand what I mean? In truth, I feel tired and confused. What I wanted to say, anyway, is that sadness in this existence is inevitable and there's no escaping it because humans accumulate desires beyond the resources of this world, and because humans are limited in capacity and with very little, and they are unable to fulfil all desires, even if the world's resources might suffice, and even if humans were capable, human desires are conflicting and it's impossible for all those desires to be fulfilled. Therefore, if there is a paradise on earth, or anywhere else in the universe, it would be unlimited in a nonsensical and fantastical way, allowing the fulfilment of all conflicting desires. Otherwise, it would be a sad paradise like this world. Honestly, I tell you, from this inhumane dungeon.

What changes when Mr. A is killed with a cold knife:

The woman who was walking calmly called out to her son for them to enter the store near him. Her fragrance was like that of ripe peaches. I remembered the days of old. The shopkeeper in the store lifted a wooden box and called out to another person taller than him who was also in the store. The woman entered after her young son and saw the man who had eaten boiled chestnuts yesterday, carrying the box, with the other man assisting him. She noticed the sweat on the man's shirt. I was about fifteen metres past the store. I stopped beside a well-known inn, whose name we prefer not to mention, frequented by workers and prostitutes dressed extravagantly and with flamboyance as if they were aristocratic ladies. A frail man with a weak build smiled at me, and I didn't pay attention. They say he works for the mayor's office, but I don't know what that means. A humble man passed by the store, wearing an ugly olive-coloured shirt, some of whose threads had frayed. His eyebrows were scattered. He had been flogged some time ago because he worked as a salt smuggler. The lady who was afraid because of what she had heard from exaggerated news about acts of violence and the killing of tax collectors in the countryside said, "Hello. Is Mr. Beranto here? He told me he might be here by 8 o'clock."

I walked across the street behind the mail truck – from which emanated the smell of horse dung – heading to the store that sells everything. When I entered the store, the scent of old artifacts was thick. The man who had eaten yesterday's boiled chestnut said, "Mr. Beranto hasn't come yet," and then fell silent. The man in the store that sells everything placed a wooden chair near me, and he said, "Please." I don't know if this was polite of him or if he was feeling bored. He asked me, "Have you heard what's going on? O, what savagery!" I replied emotionally, "Yes. What chaos, but I didn't come for that." This conversation interrupted the commotion in the street as people rushed to the spot of blood where the fat man had fallen, and the seller looked out onto the street and said, "It seems like a fight broke out." We left, and to be honest, I was happy to have something to distract me. The seller was cursing the barbaric acts that had spread among the people, and as we approached the crowd of onlookers, he looked like a mentally disturbed person. The woman who came from the countryside to work as a midwife for a family of nobles, said, as she looked distraught at what was happening, "Oh, Virgin Mary," and made the sign of the cross. The enthusiastic young man, addicted to gambling and borrowing money, as he hit his foot on the fat man's foot who had been killed, exclaimed, "They've killed him, that's for sure." The man with the worn teeth, half-drunk, said, "He's not dead, he's not dead." Make him smell money and he will kick his feet until he gets up." The man who had recently earned the title of nobility spoke fearfully, "Oh, heavens!" It wasn't amusing, nor did it provoke laughter; seeing the dead man and his dark blood was terrifying. The scent of blood mingled with the smell of women's hair who stood nearby, leather shoes, manure, the distinctive odour of chimney sweepers, and the stench of nurses treating dysentery patients. A woman removed her shawl from her head and covered the face of the deceased man with it. I wanted to return to my apartment and sleep; heaviness and silence overcame me. What does he see now? Does he know he's dead? Does he feel pain or humiliation?

I walked as if in a trance, like someone who has forgotten himself. I don't know. Hundreds have died and I hadn't seen any of them. Now, here it is, death that is fresh. It was here just moments ago, this eternal death. Has it become a venerable elder now? I imagined death like an old sage sitting atop a mountain peak, holding a thick staff. The man said to me, "Hey, aren't you paying attention?" A deep-seated fear stirred within the depths of my soul, an ancient fear since the first human, the fear of self-realisation that I won't be immortal in this world.

Among the crowd gathered around the slain – and this was strange – was Mr. Dog, whom I had previously thought would behave according to his nature and stay away from such unruly gatherings. A gathering not befitting a gentleman. I was told that he was present even before the heinous incident occurred, witnessing everything from the beginning. I recall his story among all the bystanders because it took a strange turn, filled with fabrication and exaggeration in my opinion. Because, ultimately, his neck – due to the rise of a new power after those upheavals that occurred – will end up under the guillotine, and his head will roll in the mud, and then he will close his eyes and say, "Oh, what is this?" And nobody in this whole world will assist him with everything, carrying him everywhere, I mean, holding his head, wiping his eyes when needed, scratching his nose, bringing him food without knowing where it's going, and all those things that the head of Mr. Dog needs. For all this, he'll find nothing except for his servant who has been serving him without receiving any payment from him, because he's just a head. Mr. Dog – before he became just a dog's head – was nearby, finalising a deal to sell a farm in the countryside, feeling comfortable as long as things went as he wished. He noticed, from where he was sitting, a man with an anxious look make a sudden movement towards a skinny, clumsy man, who had both sides of his face covered with the collar of his coat. He saw hands flailing but didn't hear what was being said. He became flustered and felt a sense of urgency when he saw the knife in the hand of the skinny, clumsy man. He moved his hand instinctively, wanting to stop the clumsy man. He stood in his place and shouted, "Back off! Back off!" Everyone in the coffee shop stood up, even those who only noticed after the shout of Mr. Dog.

The waiter exclaimed, "Other drinkers!" Many people gathered around the man who had fallen to the ground after the skinny, clumsy youth fled. Mr. Dog said, "Perhaps he's not dead. Isn't there a doctor here? Move back a bit." Since that ugly moment, the moment a respectable man was enjoying a good life was killed, even if it was within modest means, from that very moment, Mr. Dog has been seized by a state of bewilderment and incomprehension, and an incomplete idea about the sudden interruption of joys. He told the coachman as he returned home, "Hurry."

Mr. A, who would shortly be killed, felt uneasy as he prepared to leave, his discomfort increasing as he noticed sweat under his armpits. He reached into his inner jacket pocket, pulled out a handkerchief, and wiped his forehead. "That's enough. I'm already late," he said. In the street, movement and stillness, sound and silence, intertwined before him. A hurried woman passed by, too preoccupied to notice him. A man adjusting his trousers on the opposite pavement said, "I will not accept." A child who emerged from an alley, ran swiftly, and disappeared into another alley. A young man bumped into him, who looked at him in silence.

Mr. A opened his right hand and said, "Can't you see, you insolent?" He clenched his fist, intending to strike him forcefully. The young man retorted with historical exasperation, "This is for you, you criminal." Mr. A saw the knife in the young man's hand, panicked, and felt sweat under his armpits. The dirty nails of the young man's hand, a distorted reflection of the street on the smooth, cold surface of the knife. He stepped back, and pleadingly said, "Why? Why?" Everything felt heavy and unclear, like a surreal stone sculpture. The sound of the knife plunging into abdominal flesh. The coldness at the edge of the blade, bursts of blood vessels. A sharp and slow sound. He felt the trembling of tension in the young man's grip, the warmth of blood on the shirt, the taste of blood in his mouth. The historical exasperation. The occupying scream of the woman passing by, placing her hand over her mouth as she contemplates if anyone might stab her son with a knife. The sharp pain that caused weakness to Mr. A's legs. The knife plunged again. The smell of the sweat of the frantic young man who didn't realise until after the fifth stab. A terrible fear engulfed him, and he wished he were now hiding under the floor of an abandoned shack. Mr. A fell. Blood began to cover the ground beneath him. Nothing was moving except for some involuntary movements of the leg muscle and eyelid. Numbness before sleep, a gentle numbness spreads throughout the body, a sharp pain as if struck by a lightning bolt from the sky. His body turned colder than the surface of the knife. He said pleadingly, "What is this?" And he died, forever.

The strangeness of the story of the dog's head beheaded under the guillotine:

The sky pouring down heavy rain, the sound coming faintly inside the coffee shop, yet it reaches. The contrast between the heavy darkness and the puddles of water outside and the warm illumination inside spread among the sitters a feeling of satisfaction and tranquillity. The blend of various food aromas, the scent of wood, beverages, and women's perfumes. Oh, what memories. Well, do pleasant memories only come when we smell women's perfumes? In the coffee shop are the sounds of laughter, obscene talk, and romantic poetry, the scraping of chair legs against the floor, the clinking of cutlery on plates, the creaking of door hinges, the woman feeling the lobe of her ear. A discussion about the curvature of the Earth among three men and a woman eager to talk, repeated calls for the waiter. In the coffee house are newspapers piled up since yesterday. The man who lives in the basement sat cautiously, wishing he could slip under the table. He wasn't alone; seated at this table was also Mr. A who was killed days ago, and next to him sat the woman who lives in a crowded city, and I don't know what to say either. This is strange, for how is this woman allowed to sit in a place like this with these men? And next to the man who lives in the basement sits the young man who gazes at anklets. And on the table sat Mr. Dog, I mean the servant who continued to work without compensation had placed Mr. Dog's head on the table, and he said to him, "Sir, sir, the tongue in my mouth pains me, so I won't speak much, if you allow me, because speaking requires me to move the tongue in my mouth," – and he opened his mouth and extended his tongue to its full length – "and when it moves, it will get tired and then," – Mr. Dog said to him, I mean Mr. Dog's head, said, "May the Lord curse you! Shut up." Well, in the coffee shop, all these sat. The young man who gazed at anklets while sitting on a white chair said, "I've seen you before. You resemble..." Mr. A, who was killed, interrupted, "Come on. Come on," and opened his hands, waving, "Come on, come on, let's make up for the days we have lost." The enthusiastic woman who was discussing the curvature of the Earth said in an excited voice, "You two want to pay for me, don't you?" Mr. A said, "Let's do everything, but please, don't fight," and laughed…. The woman living in the crowded city said, "There's also no benefit in it." She felt ashamed that she wouldn't be able to pay the bill with them. The waiter's wife works hard, and that is a fact and obvious. The man in the basement thought that if he could record all the conversations that were being made, even the faint one between a gentleman and another man at the back of the coffee shop, he could write an article about the nature of coffee shops and their patrons. Mr. A spoke about the reason for their gathering here with a dull and ambiguous tone. He rubbed his nose and said, "I salute you all, the living and the dead among you." Mr. Dog felt that they were ignoring him because he is, after all, just a head, interjected, "If you'll permit me, my experience is highly sensitive because in any case, I won't die again. In truth, this is humiliating for a person who possesses a soul. You, Mr. A, are also dead, and I see this as a clear mistake. This fills me with despair." His voice began to falter and became sluggish. "Do you know what will become of me when this cursed servant dies? They'll throw me in the mud. Perhaps I will fall on my side so that one eye is in the mud, unable to see, while the other stares at the sky. This is how it has been for hundreds of years..." The servant said, "Sir... sir, even when I die, I will rise from among the dead to serve you, but you must wait for me for two or three days; perhaps I won't be able to rise from among the dead immediately after death, but if I can, I won't delay. I won't say, 'Where is the water?' Surely thirst will destroy me in the grave. Instead, I will say, 'Let me go to my master...'" Mr. Dog interrupted him, saying, "Silence! May God curse you." The young man who stares at anklets is not speaking; he looks distant with sorrow." The woman who lives in the crowded city said to herself, "Where do they get this tranquillity from when they don't have money?" The servant of Mr. Dog said, "My lord, as I said to you, I want to remain silent because the tongue in my mouth hurts me. However, I must speak when you need me. I will now shut up because you sought my silence, and as I am, as you kn..." Mr. Dog interrupted him, "You cursed being! Bring your hand near my mouth." The servant replied, "As you wish, my lord. Should I bring it closer until it touches your teeth, or should I make it..." and he extended his hand until it touched Mr. Dog's teeth. At that moment, Mr. A said, "You definitely want to bite him. Come on... Bite him like a real dog's bite. Make his eyes pop out of their sockets," and he clapped his hands and laughed. Mr. Dog snapped his teeth begrudgingly into the servant's hand for a moment. The servant said, "My lord, you're hurting me," – and he pulled his hand away – Mr. Dog, laughing, said, "Do it again, do it again. If I had clenched onto his hand any longer, he would have been pulling his hair out. There's a blessing in this servant's stupidity, but please, let's not fight nor take things too far." The man from the cellar seized this opportunity and withdrew to slip under the table. The servant said, "You must have done this intentionally, my lord. The pain that was in my tongue is gone. Look, I don't feel any pain in my tongue anymore," – and he extended his tongue covered with a white layer – "but now the pain has come into my hand. Look, my lord, blood is beginning to come out. It must be because of your bite, my lord. If it were clear to me, I would ask you to allow me to bite myself on your behalf and relieve you of..." The woman said fearfully, "Why are you talking like this? Are you ill?" Mr. A directed his question to the young man who looked at anklets, "I see you're not taking part in these joys with us. Are you sad?" The servant replied, "Am I ill, my lord? Because when I woke up this morning, I felt a little unwell, but I wasn't ill. Now, I can jump in front of you all with full strength." He then jumped several times in succession. The young man who gazed at anklets wasn't sure if he was the one being referred to by Mr. A's remarks and asked, "Oh. Are you speaking to me, sir?" Mr. A replied, "Yes, yes. You seem sad to me. You must try some things, and you will find that you're missing out on opportunities for yourself." The young anklet man said, "My soul is empty, sir, and I don't know the point of all this. As the gentleman under the table says, 'How can I be happy when what I desire will never be fulfilled?'" The busy woman thought they behaved rudely in her presence, as if she wasn't even there, so she asked, "What are the children doing now?" The basement man from under the table remarked, "There must be a place somewhere unlimited that allows for conflicting desires to be fulfilled, and that's the place that must be sought." Then he fell silent and said, "It's the eternal paradise."

The waiter's wife said something to her husband that I didn't quite hear. Mr. Dog replied, "I actually disagree with this talk coming from under the table, from my own experience, with this evident sensitivity, as I am just a head suspended in a time between natural life and death. Nothingness is the best place. Look at me now, if I were to go into nothingness after my head is severed, I wouldn't feel a thing, and I wouldn't this cursed servant, as you can see, because a place like the one you say where everything happens, even contradictory things, does not exist, and how do things happen that are contr..." Mr. A said, "Oh, these strange discussions! You're arousing my anger. Why don't you rejoice and experience things however life presents them. Here I am, I have been killed, yet I haven't lost that old inclination towards the whores. Oh God, how beautiful they are," and he laughed. Mr. Basement said, from under the table, "You don't understand, this paradise must exist." Then, "How can you be sure that nothingness exists at all?" The servant said, "My lord, the bleeding in my hands hasn't stopped. Look. I might die because of this bleeding, or perhaps feel dizzy. If I fall to the ground and spread out unable to move, everyone will go to their homes, and you'll be left here on the table with no one to carry you. I know you don't like staying here, so if you permit me, let me write my will. If I die and don't come back from among the dead, my will is for them to carry you to the nearest..." Mr. A said, "I feel bored of you all. Go on. Go on with your nonsense." Mr. Dog said: "Be quiet, please. Have mercy on me and stop talking. Don't worry about me. I'll find someone to carry me."

The busy woman said to herself, "My presence here has no value." The waiter's wife said softly, something I couldn't hear clearly, and everyone noticed the sound of the music stop. Mr. A said, "A human must be intoxicated to feel some joy, my friends, please." The distant woman's voice rose, "I think this description is good, because the sun is the one that revolves around the Earth, and because of this, the..." The voice coming from under the table said, "Alright, you've said everything." The servant said, "My lord, shall we go now? You mentioned last night that you wanted to close your eyes early. Do you understand what I mean, my lord?" The young man who stared at anklets wanted to leave. Mr. Dog, or rather Mr. Dog's head, said, "Listen. Listen. You should be a good human this time. I exempt you from all duties, but I wish from you, or I command you, because you only understand through orders. I command you to bury me, I mean bury this head. I feel bored, do you understand, you cursed one?"

Why do people talk about a dog's head? What is the point in that?

Some women I later recognised—although I don't believe it—say it's common for people to speak of a man carrying a dog's head with him everywhere. They claim he can be seen on moonlit nights in fields, forests, and mountains. He digs tirelessly, and the strikes of the pickaxe sounds from afar, like the howl of a suffering wolf. He digs incessantly, and asks, "Should I dig here, my lord? Because, my lord, if you don't tell me where to place my pickaxe with each strike, this hole will keep widening indefinitely. I've been digging for nights, and we haven't found the suitable spot yet."

The Shortcomings in the Life of Saeed Abdullah Al-...

Part I: which refers to Sir Khalid Al-Mulla and his use of the rumba rhythm as a marginal note.

Saeed Abdullah ~~Al~~ who had never slept on a bed until that night he slept in Cairo on a real bed, and who has a head as big as a cow's, and with a few minor errors from some employees that could be recorded in the livestock wealth census, is now married. He had married again.

When he was born in the late 1980s during the dry summer days, when the female lizard can be seen on the wall of the house – rented – from the inside, the father thought of naming him Mubarak, but his hesitant mother, who wrapped him in a bright yellow swaddle, said, "Marzouq." His mother, who held on to 250 Riyals wrapped in a white handkerchief in her hand, then hid it under a white-covered pillow – a cool white cover embroidered with red roses, green branches, and the phrase 'Good Morning' in a blurry Arabic script due to the needlework inaccuracy of the seamstress's hand who had embroidered the cover – put him to sleep on his back on a mattress padded with synthetic cotton. In the evening, Abdullah comes to put his face close to Saeed's face, laughs, and undoes the swaddle band, then takes off his garment – a white robe with a large sturdy collar. In the winter days, he puts his face close, then takes off a light grey jacket with black and green buttons, and he takes off black garments with a strong collar, along with black socks.

After that, he didn't sleep in the cradle—is that what you call it?—with stars and colourful cotton bears suspended from above it, while his mother slept on the ground. He didn't sit in a stroller playing birthday tunes. He slept on his back on a mattress padded with synthetic cotton.

In the mid-nineties, he sat on a wooden chair with a red adhesive backrest, rested his arms on a table whose surface peeled off in the Muadh Bin Jabal Elementary School. In those old days, he sat at the back of the classroom next to a wooden board adorned with a shiny golden frame, covered with black velvet cloth, on which ten letters of the alphabet were stuck, hastily made from coloured cardboard: ر ذ د خ ح ج ث ت ب أ (A, B, C, D, E, F, G, H, I, J). In the second row, numbers from one to ten were stuck: 1 2 3, 4 5 6, 7 8 9, 10. Every set of three numbers were painted the same colour, and the number ten was in a pale yellow colour.

It was because at first he was afraid that he didn't sit on the black leather sofa in the agent's office; he stood outside the room. On other days, he sat on the smooth wooden armrest attached above the arms of the barber's chair, on a plank placed by Maqbul the Indian who would now chew betel nut and spit out red saliva, which adorned the shelves of the wooden salon with five boxes of cheap Bigen Men's Hair Dye and bottles of Casanova Cream, and a collection of boxes full of women's facial masks, after he smeared the woman's face with a black pen. Next to the door, he hung a paper calendar with large pages, although its date had expired at least a year ago.

In the mosque, he sat beside his father and did not utter a word. At home, when his mother hung the radio on the sink to listen to the Quran broadcast, he stretched out on his back, propping his feet up on the TV stand until he dozed off. When his father raised the volume of the car radio, he would be sitting in the car's trunk. In the cramped and gloomy telephone booth, they didn't sit; they stood while speaking on the phone handset.

When they played football on the asphalt, he didn't sit; he said he was like Ali Yazid charging until the blood of his nosebleed covers the upper portion of his shirt, but they put him as goalkeeper standing between his two shoes. In school, he sat under the window on a new chair painted in soft green, in Muadh Bin Jabal Elementary School, in the counsellor's room, he didn't sit; he stood to be struck with a bamboo cane after being expelled by the teacher who said to him, "God curse you! Counsellor's room!"

He pulled it from the back of his strong-collared white robe. In the sheep pen, when his father bought an animal to slaughter, he wanted to have a taste of the water in the rusty iron trough prepared for watering the sheep. He knelt down on his knees, but then spat.

In the neighbourhood, when Muhammad ~~〰〰〰~~ came to them running, saying that America had collapsed, after watching the news of the September events on Al-Jazeera Channel, when he came to them in the middle of the afternoon, he was sitting on the steps of the Pakistani Yasin Baqoush's shop, and we only knew him by this nickname. Yassin Buqoush, who when angered says, "Alan Bock," and rises from his chair. When he became capable of stealing father's car keys, he didn't sit in the car seat; he sat in the driver's seat of the 1998 model Hilux.

In those days, Fahad Abdul Mohsen heard, "Unthuri dam'ak 'ala Al-Madi As-Saeed" (Shed your tears over the happy past), and Abdullah as-Salam heard, "Ameelu li'l-'azlah wa ab'adu 'an an-nas" (I am inclined towards isolation and I distance myself from people).

At a traffic stop, he sat cautiously and suspiciously, inhaling the comfort of dense smoke or stretching out on a shabby bed upon which a Pakistani had slept yesterday, who had accidentally ran over a Jordanian child, both in the intensive care unit. In secondary school, he sat on the footpath behind the school building to smoke. He hasn't slept on a bed until now, even when at his aunt's, he sleeps on the floor, unaware that he will sleep on a wooden bed when he travels to Cairo.

The first time he travelled, he sat in the first seat behind the driver on the public bus, but the driver told him that these seats are reserved for families. In Al-Bukhari Restaurant, he sat on the cushioned platform laid with red mats embellished with black, olive green, and orange. The Afghan boy, who attends to the customers, brought a fan near them, a charred chicken with most of its skin burnt, two servings of Bukhari rice, slices of white onion, and a bottle of hot sauce. He didn't sit on the toilet seat; in the bathroom, he squats and squirms.

He sat on a chair with a fabric cover, pieces of its yellowed padding peeking through. He sat on this chair for the clerk at the Civil Registry to take a photo of him, a picture that hardly resembled him, as he looked like a starving person. At the coffee shop, he orders grape-mulberry flavoured hookah and sits on a baliyah mat that stinks of urine, and he leans his back against the wall, where it is written in bold black letters, visible: 'Abu Adhab - Return Fahd, 6/7', and some is faintly written: 'Shaytu… What did you fill it with? - S.A.M. … Camry 2004'.

On Fridays, he doesn't sit in the mosque; he arrives at the end of the second sermon and stands waiting with the crowd. After the conclusion of the ritual prayer, he looks at the gaps in the rows and then leaves. During emergencies, like when his grandmother passed away, he sat on one of the cold, linked metal chairs. These chairs were designed in an ugly pattern to evoke a sense of fatigue in waiting. He still hasn't slept on a bed. When he applied for enrolment at King Saud University, he sat waiting in the auditorium. In the admissions and registration officer, he didn't sit. One of them said, "There are no seats left except for those in the Community College and the College of Sciences." Since the Community College does not offer a monthly stipend, he said, "College of Sciences."

In the taxi, he sat eagerly, unsure of the Camry's model driven by another Pakistani who was talking on the phone incessantly. In the rented apartment in a bachelors-only building, in a unit with two bedrooms, a kitchen integrated into the living room and a bathroom, there was an electric floor heater placed in the living room of the unit with a shelf beside it, and next to it was a tea kettle, a brass teapot, decorated white cups and saucers, plastic boxes containing tea, sugar, cardamom, ginger, and dried mint. In this apartment, he sat smoking, and drinking tea from a tea kettle painted in bright colours. In reality, he couldn't distinguish the taste of the tea whether it was Lipton or the local tasteless brand, but that's another matter.

On television, on the Al-Jazeera Channel, the same channel where Muhammad ~~Iranishal~~ saw the collapse America. He
watched what he believed to be an academic delivering a racial-
ly charged speech against women and black men, from that distant figure. Muhammad didn't remember, but he was surprised
and felt a mix of satisfaction and tension because someone noticed and documented this event. In those days, he heard and
old favourite by Khalid Al-Mulla. He ate from McDonald's,
not on a dining table, but sitting on the ground or in the car
seat when he went out with Youssuf ~~devithing~~.

In the apartment with the electric floor heater, he felt nostalgia and frustration. In Hail, he used to attend artistic gatherings during breaks to see the percussionist Abu Haider perform,
regardless of who was singing, whether it was Khalid Al-Salama
or a novice artist. Abu Haider, who plays five rhythms at same
time, has in his mind a blurry image representing all that is
beautiful and sublime. It is was only once that he had sat directly behind Abu Haider, and now he feels nostalgia and frustration in the apartment, watching Abu Haider on YouTube
and pressing the like button. In the Deanship of Admissions
and Registration, when he left the university, he didn't sit, he
didn't sit in any office. He sat on a wooden bench and then
pulled out his file. Until now, he hasn't sat on any couch in
a bank, nor on any metal or wooden chair in Alrajhi Bank.
But after Isha ritual prayer, which he hadn't performed, he sat
on the pavement, mindful of his wooden-soled shoes that he
had bought three days ago. In those days when he used to sit
on the grass after playing in a hired field, he bought an olive
jacket adorned with yellow buttons for 300 Riyals. He didn't
sit in the store; he stood in front of the mirror. In his entire

life, he had never bought a jacket more expensive than this one. While in the lounge, on the floor, he played Baloot and smoked. Queen of Trumps, Jack of Trumps, Seven of Spades, Ten of Diamonds, Queen of Diamonds on the floor, King of Trumps: Diamonds are the Trump Suit. Ten of Clubs, Nine of Clubs, Jack of Clubs, Ace of Diamonds, Eight of Trumps, on the floor is Ten of Diamonds: He did not say, "San," but said, "Pass." In the second instance, he said, "Clubs are the Trump Suit," then on casting his first card, he said, "Sira."

In the evening, on a cool soft bed, he lies on his stomach and bends his leg until his knee rises to the level of his chest or close to it, drinking water and taking off his long trousers. Then he lies down again and bends his leg. In sleep, he did not see himself sitting at a home dining table spangled with white ceramic plates, shiny silver knives and spoons, nor did he see himself sleeping on a white bed in a room with large windows in a hotel in Mykonos, where a girl who graduated from the Philosophy Department works at the reception, because he is from the middle class or lower-middle class, because that is how he also saw himself in a classroom where his feet were numb from the impact of the desk, surrounded by little children singing: "Black, black, fell and injured his head."[1] He was sad in the dream because the supervisor hit him again after being angry about the commotion caused by the students, twisting in helplessness and submission, trying to avoid the supervisor's cane in vain.

---

1. This is a modified version of a Kuwaiti traditional song from the 1970s. The original song says: Bald, bald fell and injured his head. [أقرع مقيرع طاح بط راسه] [Translator]

When he woke up, he sat up straight, his legs on a cold and soft bed. He drank come water, and remembered that he heard in the dream: "Black, black, he knocked over the bowl."

Back home, when he sat on the floor and drank the second cup, after hearing a scolding from his mother, he said, "I will enrol in the Faculty of Hospitality and Tourism."

It was in his second year at college that he slept for the first time on a bed, a real bed. He attended Abdullah's ~~third~~ wedding and then travelled to Cairo. In the December cold, he slept on a bed in a rented apartment in Dokki. A driver had rented it for them whose number they had acquired from Ibrahim Al-Asfar, a driver who works as a pimp and uses his own car, transporting arrivals from the airport to any apartment in Cairo. He told them, "It will cost 400 Egyptian Pounds," then he spoke about another apartment that is safer, costing 600 Egyptian Pounds. He said, "I could settle it for 550 Egyptian Pounds."

On the first day, he did not stay up late; they walked and ate food on Jamia Al-Duwal Street. On the second day, he sat on a couch that emitted the smell of cleaners; he was too embarrassed to tell them about his desire to drink wine, a glass of delicious red wine, as he thought.

He drank beer with a passion, then he saw that the women were ugly because their shiny eyebrows were drawn with black pens, the women whom the driver brought, who showed obnoxious flattery. The women who had white powder on their faces and necks. The woman whose belly he saw shaking as they got on the bed where he would later sleep. And he saw stretch marks on her upper thighs. As he sat on the edge of the bed, looking at his black socks that reached mid-calf, elastic black socks, the woman who sweated at the base of her back wiped her armpits with fidgetingly.

It was because he felt cold that he sat on the ground, in front of him were the food bags they had ordered, and he wrapped himself in the red blanket adorned with illustrations of a spotted leopard, smoked, and felt boredom and guilt. "I won't try it again the next night." He saw his other friend coming out naked and loud. The other woman said something foul as she returned her lipstick to her bag, and lit a cigarette from the cigarette packet on the table in front of the couch, which gave the fragrance of cleaners. When everything was over, he felt regretful and drank a beer.

On the third day, they sat at a dining table, a real dining table. When the Zuhr call to ritual prayer came, he didn't hear it. When he woke up, he woke up to a sharp pain in his throat, and he said it was very cold. In the taxi, he sat sluggishly in the back seat, and in a restaurant called ⬛⬛ , the three of them sat at a dinner table. After they got out of the taxi in Salah Salem, he sat on a wooden chair, staring at distant green bushes. He didn't feel like eating, hesitated to drink water because he knew it would irritate his throat even more. The cold air passed gently. He said to his friend, "Let's buy some Panadol." They had fine meat, but he didn't care. When it was time for Maghrib ritual prayer, he heard the sound of the muezzin's hand knocking on the microphone, then heard the sound of the man moving away. In the apartment, on the couch that smelled of smoke and buttery odour, he stretched out and crossed his legs, tucking his feet under his buttocks, because he felt pain in his knee joints and a headache. He now knew that the cold had started since morning. That night and the following four nights, he didn't see any shiny eyebrows drawn with black pens or stretch marks on the skin. He heard a voice reaching him, softly like a sunbeam. He heard laughter, while lying on his stomach in bed, feeling pain in the back of his throat, a headache like buzzing, joint pain, and a temperature. What does Panadol do? From time to time, they both ask him if he can come down with them. Then they ask him if he can at least stay up with them in the living room. When he heard the girl say, "I'm joking with you," and she laughed, his spirits lifted, and he wanted to get up to see her saying this phrase, but he felt too tired to get up to urinate, then he fell asleep. Then he spent the next night sleeping, and so on.

He sat in the back seat with the driver feeling disappointed and exhausted, all of them heading to the airport. At Gate 4, they sat on the chairs of a coffee shop called ▩▩. In seat L30, which he obtained at a discounted price because it was non-refundable, he said, "Next time, Syria; I hate Egypt."

Days later, at Alrajhi Bank, he sat on a chair with its stale yellow cotton padding covered with black fabric. The clerk said to him, "Sign."

At home, he at as his mother cut the orange, the orange whose scent wafted through her clothes, and some of the droplets of its juice fell on the white china plate, he mentioned that they were offering him a job at a branch of Mobily on Airport Road. His father, who adjusted his headscarf, said, "Ma Sha Allah," and felt pleased. In late afternoon, those days, he felt annoyed by the work pressure, dealing with papers, various clients, and veiled women, unsure if they applied white powders to their faces and necks, the computer screen, sitting on a fine chair. But he couldn't find good company in the office. Saud was noisy and ostentatious, wearing socks printed with images of domestic animals. Abdulaziz Al-Adi, the branch manager, sits in a room with glass walls, writing something, and he smiles when he passes by. His headscarf is red. The security guard, whose shirt collar had wilted and showed signs of white sweat stains, doesn't sit down; he's from the lower-middle class or lower still, so he remains standing. There were others I didn't recognise.

After those days, sitting on the floor at home, he told his father, who was drinking coffee from a cup decorated with golden patterns and felt the need to go to the bathroom, he told him optimistically: "I'm going to quit my job at Mobily because I've been tentatively accepted for the administrative job offered to me in company, an administrative job where I'll sit on a fixed black chair, at a Chinese-made desk of compressed wood." Father, sitting in his place inside the rented house, didn't say, "Ma Sha Allah." Instead, he said, "Wonderful, by Allah." He added, "I think their salaries are around 7,600." Father replied, "Masha Allah."

In the evening, the mother cut with her knife whose handle is green, a sweet red apple, and the father quietly and gratefully drank tea. After his stool and urine had been tested, he sat on a sturdy black chair at a Chinese desk on the ground floor of the administration. In front of him sat another man, at another Chinese desk, who had reached the end of his fifties, who did nothing. In the following days, he was surprised because everyone seemed to enjoy a mysterious indifference. In the signature room, he signed documents while standing, but his signature didn't look like his usual one when he sat on the chair at the Alrajhi Bank. He signed in the form of the Arabic letter 'A' and enclosed it within a circle. At the bank, he sat on the edge of the soft leather couch because he wanted a loan, the maximum, to buy a car on instalments instead of using his father's car to go to work, and for marriage later on.

In the evening, leaning his back against sturdy and heavy backrests, he said, "We are hiring an Ethiopian woman." Mother said, "These black women are no good." After handing over a cup of red tea, she added, "They kill children."

When the woman, whom Mother thought would have a heavy scent, arrived at the international lounge at ~~King~~ airport, she had come wearing a loose green dress with cotton pants underneath, clinging to her legs. She carried a black bag in her hand and looked around quickly and hesitantly. At home, Mother saw that her health was good and she had a strong body. In truth, there was no indication that she might be sick or that she kills children, and her mind was sound, except that she believed in a deity that had been struck on his back and spat in his face. When she used salt excessively with the dishwashing liquid, Mother said in explanation and desperation, "You don't understand." In those joyful days, the black woman arranged the new sofa they bought for 2,500 Riyals so they could place it in the living room. Mother's spirit was joyful, and she wanted to invite her neighbours to sit on it, drink tea, and see it with their own eyes. When everyone sat on the sofa, which barely fit through the narrow door of the house, Mother said, "We want to paint the living room and the women's room."

Father said, "Get married, son." After countless trips between work and the rented house, sitting in the driver's seat in a Toyota car, the mother thought about her niece; he wouldn't marry a bedouin girl whose father worked as an assistant in the Agriculture Department or worked in General Intelligence with the rank of sergeant, nor would he marry a fair-skinned girl studying dentistry from a family whose ancestor was a Turkistani. She thought of her niece, her niece who sleeps on a bed, graduated from university specialising in Arabic Language, black but not dark-skinned, a subtle yellowish glow could be seen on her nose and cheeks, curly hair that can be straightened with keratin, not obese, when she wears jeans, she becomes beautiful. Anyway, she is a girl and acceptable, and before all of this, she is her niece and obeys her.

Saeed said he didn't want the Samari dance this night, and said that using the using the electronic keyboard with the daf was an ugly act, and wished if Khalid Al-Mulla would perform that night and sing songs to the rumba rhythm. Oh God, if that were possible. On that night, in the middle of the hall next to his aunt's husband, he sat on a wide wooden chair decorated with golden engravings, stood up to greet and took with his right hand the white envelope written on it in Hazel font: 'Many congratulations, dear Uncle!' In the courtyard of the guest palace, a fire was lit to warm up for the aviation. After dinner, the black men sat in two rows facing each other, the sound of the drum was sharp and poignant. The obese man who moved between the rows to instruct them, his voice came out strong among the rhythm and the voices of the black men, like a commander directing his battalion before death, moving his hands to enthuse them: shaking the baton, nodding, tuning his turns, and so on. In the hotel, he sat, after taking off his black cloak embroidered with golden threads.

After those days, when he sat in the new rented apartment, he did not have many children like his father did. The couple hadn't even conceived until that night when they parted ways. Days passed for them quietly, without much understanding of most things. They sat on a red velvet couch in their new rented apartment and slept on a wide bed with soft white covers. A large golden chandelier hung above them, emitting soft light. They stood in the kitchen, she was washing the few dishes and he stood watching the boiling of the electric kettle. They sat on chairs in some restaurants, and they sat at her father's house a few times. She sat alone in the evening, while he played Baloot and didn't respond. She didn't hit him with the new egg frying pan, nor did they stand on the staircase of the building arguing, nor did he pull her by her hair, and what else can we say? In reality, nothing of those things happened, which when we recall them, we say emotionally: 'God-forbid, why?' Everything was calm and happening in an undefined mystery. He smoked while she watched a delicate white actress on television playing the role of a woman dedicating her life to work. On the laptop, he played: 'Ujaadhibuka al-hawa,' sung by Khalid Al-Mulla, and played Baloot. He wasn't happy, and her spirit wasn't joyful. As for her, there was no other choice for her.

After sitting on the edge of the bed uncountable times, and after laying on his back next to her numerous times, he divorced her. He divorced his maternal aunt's daughter, the cousin with whom he had slept on the floor.

He paid the rent for the new apartment and sat on the floor with Mother who silently cut the cold oranges. He didn't give Father a clear answer when he asked him about the reason for the divorce, and Father was speaking angrily. He said, "I wasn't comfortable," or, "I didn't love her," or, "We didn't agree," and so on, without speaking about her sharp features, nor did he speak ill of her. It was something distant, as the mother thought. In those days, when the maid who worships Allah, besides Whom there is no god, put down the tea pot, he said he would marry someone from Jordan. Mother, who was saddened because her sister was no longer the same, from the kitchen said, "You brought a gypsy to us."

After his delayed application for permission to marry a foreigner, he sat on a comfortable chair in Alrajhi Bank. In Amman, he sat in the company of that man on a wooden chair painted dark brown in Abu Jbara Restaurant, in the smoking section, and drank tea. In the evening, he didn't play Baloot. He sat in the home of the family that his daughter would later marry into. It was a family I had some connection to. On the floor, he sat humbly and anxiously in the men's gathering, while the man accompanying him sat confidently. Afterwards, they had a brief dinner celebration. He married a white girl who had no choice; she hadn't graduated from the Arabic Language Department at the university. She was from a family I had an old connection with through one of my relatives there. By God, they were not tramps. He shook hands with the mother, who kissed his hands and head. As they returned from Amman and Tabuk, and he was frequently travelling between the two, she sat in the back seat, tense from the driver's handling and from life, speaking in whispers. He sat in the back seat, the man accompanying him next to the driver, eager for it to end. During those days, they didn't sit with Mother who was cutting oranges; they sat in the newly rented apartment. Father prepared a brief dinner in honour of the wife who wasn't from among gypsies.

He sat in countless places, though all those places he sat in indirectly indicated that he belonged to the middle class, but not the lower-middle class. Some of the places he sat in hinted that his wife was Jordanian and not from among tramps. After sitting on the edge of the bed countless times, they were blessed with a dark-skinned daughter and a beautiful-eyed son. They hesitated about going to Amman. His wife went with the children. He sat on the chair at his work desk. He sat at his father's funeral.

They sat with Mother who was cutting oranges joyfully with her grandchildren. And so, even in those days he spent laid in the mortuary at the hospital ᵥₐₙₙ, he did not feel the cold. He also lay in the grave and did not sit.

Part II: which refers to the aesthetics of Sir Khalid Al-Mulla with the aim of influencing the reader.

He does not remember whether he heard a guest with Abir Nasraoui on Radio Monte Carlo or read on a musical instrument website that the greatness of Khalid Al-Mulla is embodied in his authenticity. Khalid Al-Mulla relies on a heritage of Adeni and Hadrami singing, and does not limit himself to the market; this allows him to express his artistic nature, in addition to his high aesthetic taste. It suffices that he chose from all of Faisal Al-Zenkawi's songs the song 'Amma al-An' [Nowadays] released by Al-Zenkawi in the mid-1980s. Saeed Abdullah, while listening to the long conversation on Radio Monte Carlo radio about Khalid Al-Mulla wanted to   and to memorise this part. He intends to say it to Isa when they stroll late at night while listening to 'Ba'adti 'Anni' in the voice of Al-Mulla. He will pause the recording and speak as if he himself were personally the subject of the matter. He said that Khalid Al-Mulla does not care about what the market demands like ̶X̶X̶X̶X̶X̶X, and he may refer to his song choices and compare between Al-Mulla's choice of Al-Zenkawi's song 'Amma al-An' and ̶X̶X̶ choice of the song 'Wahda bi-Wahda'.

He tells this in a naive tone, imagining himself as a guest in the Monte Carlo studio speaking in front of Abir Nasraoui or as a writer on a musical instrument website. He restarted the recording, turned to face Isa as if he had just achieved a victory, "Now you know why Abu Hannan [Al-Mulla] is great?" He nods confidently because he knew Khalid Al-Mulla from long ago. As for Isa, about whom we know nothing except that he will die because he preferred to save a larger amount for travel rather than buying new tires for his car, which turned into scrap after a bad accident. As for Isa, he calmly says, as if wanting to spoil the matter, "Al-Mulla is great because he inspires you." Saeed wiped the corner of his eye with a steady finger, a steady black finger. He passed the side street he wanted, and Isa told him to turn with the next side street, and he pointed to the red sign of the refrigeration and air conditioning shop with his hand. The red sign had yellow lettering that read, 'For refrigeration and air conditioning (air conditioners - refrigerators - washers - ovens - vacuum cleaners), the owner Hamoud Al-Anzi'. Isa remarked, somewhat sarcastically, that we wouldn't hear him ask Mubarak to stop pretending to forget the life he had lived, and he reminded him of an embarrassing incident associated with this street and laughed. Saeed responded apologetically with another quip that we wouldn't hear him, apologising that he didn't forget the neighbourhood, but he didn't notice the street. As the car passed near Ayyash

Al-Shi'ei's house, when the car passed by the humble white house with its green iron gate, Saeed asked if the Ayyash family had moved, saying he remembered the young children. Devils, my brother. The truth is, when Saeed saw the humble white house, he remembered the little boy, a small child standing at the green iron gate. Every time Saeed passed by it, walking nearby, he heard him calling out, "Bassindana!" and pointing to him. Saeed, who was passing by, didn't understand what 'Bassindana' meant. But he would later understand without intending to say: 'Badhinjaana (Eggplant)' and pointed to him. This is what Saeed remembered when he said, "Devils, my brother." He stopped the car. Isa wanted to light a cigarette, and said that he might go to Kuwait for the wedding of Mubarak, his paternal uncle's son. Saeed, seizing the opportunity, said, "Ma Sha Allah, his circumstances have improved." Isa said decisively, "If you come with me, we will attend an event for Al-Mulla." He wanted to tell a story that came to his mind now before he got out, perhaps hoping Saeed would agree to accompany him if he knew that Mubarak frequented Al-Mulla's sessions. Saeed said, "God willing." Eagerly, Isa mentioned that Mubarak had told him he heard Khalid Al-Mulla telling a story in the presence of Aboud Khawaja. Mubarak was among the attendees when Khalid Al-Mulla said that. In the 1970s, Al-Mulla worked in the reception of hospital ~~Amman~~. At that time, Al-Mulla had released two albums and gained some fame, but the albums were released without his picture on the cover, so the listener recognised only his name and voice.

Al-Mulla narrated as Mubarak heard: "I received a call from a nurse working in the sixth ward, asking about the duty manager. When I answered, she recognised the voice and asked to make sure if it was me, the Al-Mulla who sings?" Al-Mulla, who expressed a mixture of pleasure and anxiety, said, "Yes, I am the Al-Mulla who sings," and winked at the person sitting next to him at the reception, tilting his head. Her curiosity and admiration for Al-Mulla's voice prompted her to boldly ask about his appearance. Al-Mulla casually commented on the beauty of his voice and indicated hesitantly and without confirmation that he was white with long hair. She began to repeat her calls during Al-Mulla's duty hours. Eventually, she requested to see him, saying, "Come to the sixth ward, but don't speak to me. You'll recognise me by my black shoes, because all the nurses in the ward adhere to the official dress code, which requires them to wear white shoes." Al-Mulla, who was apprehensive yet intrigued to see this caller who kept repeating her calls, said, "Alright." Without hesitation, he said to the young man with long white hair who was working with him in the Inquiries Department, "Come, let me show you something." He took him to the sixth ward and said to him, "Take a look at who's wearing black shoes." He looked but saw nothing apart from gleaming white footwear, so they returned to their department. When the black phone with small buttons rang, Al-Mulla quickly answered because he knew she would call, and he said to her, "I came, yet I didn't see any nurse wearing black shoes." She laughed and said, "So it's you? I saw you." With embarrassment, she admitted that she had seen him before in the Inquiries area and had wished it was him before she had even seen him. She then daringly and reproachfully asked, "Why did you bring this nigga with you?" Al-Mulla laughed heartily, mimicking her manner of questioning. Aboud Khawaja, who was sitting and listening to Al-Mulla telling his story from the seventies, laughed, and he laughed loudly. That's how Mubarak recounted it. Isa, who was narrating this story while sitting in Saeed's car, got out and smoked. Saeed Abdullah ~~too~~ laughed as well, bidding Isa farewell, agreeing to meet again in the evening. If things went as planned, he would travel to Kuwait in winter via Al-Qassim–Hafar Al-batin road, attending the Samri[1] for Mr Khalid Al-Mulla.

---

1. A traditional folk dance performed with by men and women, and accompanied by singing. It is famous in Arab Gulf Countries. [Translator]

Vollmer Brecht,
or the Government Employee

Nobody knows Vollmer Brecht, this single forty-year-old who resides in a small and modest apartment in the heart of Berlin, except by his description as a low-ranking government employee in an unknown government department. It can be said without any sense of fallacy that Vollmer is the ultimate embodiment of the idea of a person being a government employee. I know that history is long, and the phrase 'ultimate embodiment' is unreasonable, but I insist on its accuracy. I don't mean by any means that he is an example of a model employee who adheres to work schedules in attending and leaving, works as necessary for the job's interest, even at the expense of his comfort, does not allow personal problems to affect his mood at work, executes instructions higher up even if he doesn't understand their justification, like a typewriter under the hand of a quick clerk that works with diligence and patience. He feels guilty if he doesn't go to work due to an illness that afflicts him suddenly, which improves after hours. All these situations are what a strict manager would expect who isolates himself in his office. This is all a marginal historical embodiment of the idea, ending with retirement or a major problem occurring at work that drives the employee to resign or engage in actions detrimental to the job as revenge against his manager. Vollmer was far from that. He saw this world as a large governmental circle; he did not understand his existence except as a government employee. I mean he was the epitome of a government employee – akin to the economic man and suchlike expressions – he did nothing in his life except to be a government employee, whether during work hours, on holidays, or even when drinking in a bar, smoking a hand-rolled cigarette, eating yesterday's dinner as today's lunch, speaking about war with a group of men he didn't know, or even when he walks on the footpath with boredom and without intending a specific destination, he was nothing but a low-ranking government employee.

Berlin was a miserable version of hell, and even if it were pure hell, it could have been understood in some way, but the appalling way in which the beauty of things collapsed, was due to the war. It placed people walking on the street under unbearable pressure, a pressure only borne by those who had lost their minds because they did not realise the extent of the horror that was taking place. Yet, Vollmer could understand this miserable situation without losing his mind. He saw what was happening as nothing more than an inescapable administrative inevitability that must be executed precisely and according to instructions. The war did not pose any humanitarian problem for him; what bothered him was only that it had personally affected him when the manager of the government department he worked for announced the cessation of work, as the clerks of the Correspondence Department passed by the offices announcing the manager's request in rapid strides, past the doors of the offices without any of them looking at who was inside,

"General meeting... general meeting," they said, even though it was not part of their job duties. Within minutes, the employees gathered in the foyer of the large building, which consisted of four floors with many windows crowding its facade. They assembled in a seemingly unintentional, yet orderly manner, with department heads in the front rows accompanied by their office staff, followed by other employees arranging themselves in hierarchical fashion. Vollmer stood at the back, upon his toes, turning his head from side to side, stretching his neck, hoping to catch a glimpse of the manager as he spoke. The manager's nervousness was evident as he improvised his speech, talking much about the resilience of the army, his words punctuated by the enthusiastic applause of the employees and his observance of their empty faces. At the end of his speech, his voice barely reaching Vollmer, the manager said, "We have served our country diligently throughout our days of work, and now the time has come for this work to stop. Such are the orders that have come from the leadership." Vollmer seized upon something regarding work stopping and quickly tapped the shoulder of the man in front of him. "What is he saying? How can work stop?" he asked. The man replied, leaning down to him to make him hear over the cheering that hailed the Fuhrer's words. "I will be going to Duisburg," he said, "I have received a letter from my paternal aunt saying that things are fine over there, and she does not say anything meaningless." Vollmer realised that work was over, and this reality, which he had never considered, not even once, crushed him. In fact, he feared contemplating what would happen to him after retirement. I say, this reality crushed him because all the supposed respect that people should have offered to a worker like him, all the greetings he received on rare occasions, and he remembers their details, the envious glances from his colleagues at work if he was thanked by the office manager, and all the words of gratitude from the clients he served, all of this was crushed under the feet of the military who, in their foolishness, caused the work to stop, making him feel a terrible sense of contempt.

Since that moment when Vollmer was no longer a low-ranking government employee in an unknown government department, he has been living a difficult life. Anyone who sees him realises that he is suffering from a mental illness. He had become terrifying emaciated. In fact, his appearance was utterly repulsive; perhaps he hadn't changed his clothes in weeks. He doesn't eat any food unless there's barely enough to eat, and even then, it's only on rare occasions. Days pass by while he consumes nothing but canned cabbage pickles in a box he found on a shelf in the kitchen of the apartment opposite his, which belonged to a lady he knew from a brief encounter to be a teacher, and whom the gestapo had arrested. Vollmer would enter the building's apartments searching for anything useful since the building was empty of its residents after those who could leave Berlin had left. Others, either the airstrikes had killed them, the gestapo had arrested them, or they were hiding in shelters. On one occasion, while he was searching for food in an apartment on the upper floor which an elderly doctor and his wife inhabited, he heard a loud explosion and felt a tremor that knocked him onto his face. He quickly realised upon descending that the explosion was just a howitzer shell that had struck the wall of his apartment. It had left a hole in the wall and fine grey dust covering everything. Due to this hole, he could no longer sleep in his apartment. He started sleeping on the wooden bed of the chatty old lady from whom he rented his apartment. Once he got used to it, he moved his typewriter, papers, the box of pickled cabbage that had only a little left in it, a few dried fruit boxes, and his two coats that he would wear one on top of the other, to the old chatty lady's apartment, determined to settle there because of its warmth, as he kept reassuring himself when he first entered. The apartment was neatly arranged in a way that gave him a sense of reassurance. The walls were adorned with paintings of respectable ladies, and on the fireplace mantel, there were sculptures of artistic value carved from wood and other metals that he couldn't identify. The room doors were of warm, brown colour, adorned with prominent intricate patterns that he could feel with his hand. The windows overlooking the street had heavy curtains in cheerful colours. In the midst of all this, you could see a plush green velvet sofa that could accommodate three people comfortably, and a small bookcase with four shelves filled with books that had never been opened, as far as he could tell. The furniture pieces were arranged so precisely that it made him feel as if the apartment was built as a single piece and no part of the furniture could be separated from it. Vollmer always sat on the green sofa in front of the fireplace, which he only managed to light on a few occasions as he couldn't find any firewood and ended up burning some timber and old books. He would sit and place his typewriter on a short table in front of him and write. He would write things he intended to present to his manager earnestly, imagining once that he had discovered a solution to the employees' tedium, but he later dismissed this idea, focusing instead on what he called the 'bureaucracy problem'. He would write on things like these in his early days until he ran out of paper. Then he didn't know what to do next. Sometimes, he would observe the street through the window in obnoxious silence, as if someone was expecting an important answer from him, and he remained silent. Only the sounds of B-17 bomber planes and alarm sirens meaninglessly break through this silence. If he turned sharply to the corner, he could see the hospital, completely destroyed, and the row of houses turned into rubble. On the other side, he could see a large anti-aircraft gun erected in the middle of the street, surrounded by sandbag piles, manned by nine Hitler Youth, enthusiastic teenagers with no military training. Only a burning tramcar separated them from Vollmer. Fires raged everywhere in Berlin, and smoke columns rose infinitely, as if they too wanted to escape to the sky and never return. There were no civilians in sight except for the dead, whose corpses decayed on the footpaths and amidst the small puddles left by the rain. Even the dogs died on the pavement. He watched all of this with indifference, waiting for the war to end so he could return to his job. Occasionally, he briefly entertained the thought that his residence in the apartment that he does not return to might exceed its lease, and he would have to apologise when the old talkative lady returned.

On the morning of one of the cold days, that chill that reminds you of bleak things, Vollmer had huddled into himself wearing his coat, and wrapped himself in a heavy woollen blanket. He awoke to the sound of a powerful noise coming from the street, the beating sound of soldiers from a mechanised infantry unit of the Soviet Army crossing the street in front of his window. He saw them from behind the curtains, walking steadily and resolutely, singing. He knew that Berlin had finally fallen into their hands. He hurried to the large mirror in the room of the lady who owned the apartment, which towered over the decorative table, and stood before it to tidy up his appearance. His beard was thick and dirty, and his moustache had grown so long that it covered his lips, his eyes were sunken and bloodshot, as if they were acutely inflamed. He wiped his face with his hands after wetting them with his saliva, and he struck his coat in the dirty spots until he thought he had done the best he could in these conditions. He stepped out into the street, and the soldiers passed by him without noticing his presence. He walked quickly to catch up with them, and when he was beside one of the soldiers, he said as he walked, "I'm a government employee. I've worked for a long time and I can work with you. I don't know how to use a weapon, but I do administrative work." The soldier gestured to him with his hand as if shooing away a fly and uttered a word that Vollmer didn't understand. He stopped and then returned to speak to another soldier, "I'm good at writing, test me. Please, sir." The soldier looked at him, and Vollmer repeated, "Writing," moving his fingers downward as if typing on a typewriter. The soldier pointed his rifle at him as he walked towards Vollmer, who stepped back slowly, raising his hands in surrender.

The Skill of Choosing a House that Americans Cannot Bomb

A

At 9 or 11 o'clock, the air conditioner strokes your forehead whenever the air wave moves downward, in a typical and gentle motion. The air is refreshing and immersive. You sit down to drink tea with excessive relaxation, in comfortable oblivion of time. Light up a cigarette if you're a smoker. Don't worry, as long as you limit the number of cigarettes you smoke, you won't get lung cancer. Sometimes, you won't suffer lung cancer even with unlimited smoking – note that cancer is known to be an unlimited cellular division and growth – drink your tea, stretch your legs after feeling tingling and cramping. Be reassured that your son is in his room with his soft index finger flipping through YouTube on his mother's mobile phone, but this son of yours is actually in his room messing around with the almost new hair trimmer you bought from Amazon, and perhaps he cut some of his hair and cried. You blame your wife as you both lie in bed. She tells you she wants to sleep but she wanted to say that the matter doesn't need all this fuss. Later, you shave your son's hair evenly. You drink the red tea from a cup with no handle, remembering that you saw such cups in the TV series 'Al-Hayalah' and liked them, but you're mistaken, in the 'Al-Hayalah' series, Dawas Bin Alef drinks red tea with a cup having a handle at the Nawab Coffeehouse. Yahya Al-Shahri – your tight underwear annoys you – passes the ball across the field on the Sports Channel 1, so it's not 11 o'clock as we also thought. Think: Can you go to the lounge, delay the time, or does excessive relaxation and the wedding invitation card that you threw at your feet after reading it prevent you from thinking about going out? You must wait for your wife to accompany her to the wedding hall. Your wife, who is now checking her hair and waiting for her sister's reply on WhatsApp. A shiny white card with a silver frame, with prominent letters: 'Honourable Flight Commander ... Sons of the late Sheikh Qablan ... are pleased to invite you to the wedding of our son, Engineer Badr ... to the daughter of Major General Mohsen ...' On the way, you tell her to return with her brother or to consider her situation carefully. Abu Saud, who is holding his mobile phone now and bringing it close to his ear, his ear, which has grown ugly hair on the skin of its cartilage, and is full of oozing wax, asks you to come to the lounge because tonight is hot. Dinner is fried saijan fish and white rice. Do you know why he insists on inviting you? He wants to compensate for last night's loss, he feels a bitterness that doesn't show. If Al-Hadari Abdul Razzaq hadn't told him, "You fool, you've wasted the trump card (kaboo¹t)," and hadn't slapped the cards on the

---

1. Kaboot: In a game of Baloot, when any player from the two teams gains the highest point available, they say, "Kaboot". [The Author]

ground, maybe he wouldn't feel the hidden bitterness, and he wouldn't remind you of the fried saijan. So don't play, and tell him you don't play against a rookie. Abu Saud is weak-minded, or so it seems. By God, there's something in his mind, but I can't pinpoint it. It's not unlikely that he's like Mu'arrid – who is from the Jerir tribe – when his brothers went to fight and left him with their family. They said to him, "You will stay with our women, so they won't be taken captive." When his brothers left, he came to the women and their children, so he brought them to an uncovered well and had a narrow opening at the top but a wide floor, and he threw them in. Then he took a lab of rock and closed the mouth of the well with it. He then followed his brothers, and when he caught up with them, they asked him why he had left their women, and he informed them of what he did. They came back and took them out of the well, but some of them had died. Some of them were on the verge of dying from hunger and distress.

Abu Saud, whose ear wax oozed and the doctor at the Ear, Nose, and Throat Clinic did nothing but give him ear drops and told him, "Come back after two or three days, I forgot."

This Abu Saud is not unlikely to be like Mu'arrid, except that he won't fight. Sometimes, when he gets annoyed by the stupidity of some of the talk he hears in the lounge and his palm sweats, feeling his muscles incapable of bearing its excess weight, he articulates his eternal objection question, which was found with the first bureaucrat clerk who gave him his salary, "If the salary stops, how will we live?" He utters 'live' with calm confidence, echoing from thirty-six worlds of scholars of the Shiah, the Jahmiyyah, the Mu'tazilah, and five from the people of the Sunnah, and I forgot who else." However, he will not fight, and if conscription is mandated – and I imagine this from my perspective because conscription has not been legalised so far – he will obtain a medical report proving that he suffers from rheumatism, excessive weight, shortness of breath, baldness, occasional stiffness, vitiligo, and an incomprehensible wife. Abu Saud sits in the lounge area. He is its master, in truth. Who called you and asked you about the saijan fish? Who buys the sugar and tea? Who buys the roasted coffee beans from Al-Marwani Roastery? Who renews the subscription for Bein Sports through a Kuwaiti person even though he doesn't care about football? He bought playing cards, the same ones he lost with yesterday. Abu Saud is generous, no matter what we say. He's truly generous, by God. If the funds allocated for the lounge run out, he doesn't wait, he buys everything he needs on credit, which he pays at the end of the month, saying, "How can we live without it?" Abu Saud, who left his house in the middle of late afternoon; who fathered their first child with his wife eight years after their marriage; Abu Saud, who sold his land for forty thousand, gave up supporting Al-Ittihad since the days of Al-Hassan Al-Yami, and if he sees a black Al-Ittihad player on the sports channel, he asks, "Is that Hamza Idris?"

After watching the match, after dinner, and after a cup of red tea sweetened with sugar, he engages in arguments about anything that's said. He reads some strange news from his Twitter account and comments on them, then says, "No... no... It turns out it's old news." He feels embarrassed, and his muscles feel weak. Abdul Razzaq Al-Hadari opposes him at every word he says because Abu Saud won't fight when mocked; instead, he becomes laughable. His white face turns red, he moves his hands about, and some drops of urine he's unaware of drip out. He gets angry but doesn't puff up, yes, he doesn't puff up. His voice rises as he repeats his arguments interruptingly, and Abdul Razzaq laughs, interjects him, and raises his voice to infuriate him. Don't be surprised if I tell you that he doesn't puff up, and don't think I'm exaggerating, because in your life, you've never seen someone who puffs up. Well, yesterday or the day before yesterday, we played a game of Baloot. Abdul Razzaq the Contemptible played with Abu Saud, and I played with the doctor. Abu Saud, playing Baloot with the cards he had bought, caused us to lose the game by 'Fooling the Baloot' because he didn't play the Ace of Diamonds, which he was retaining with his short, pointed fingers. Al-Hadari Abdul Razzaq got upset and said, "You fool! You wasted the Ace of Trumps card!" and he threw the card on the ground. He tackled Abu Saud – while both of them were sitting down – and pinned him down, and rode on top of him, saying, "Play your Ace! Play your Ace!" and I swear by God, I burst out laughing. Abu Saud struggles like a sea lion trying to rise, and I did not say 'like a seal', but like a sea lion. When Abdul Razzaq released him, he didn't get up, felt a bitterness that didn't show, and his jaws failed to lift the sea lion. But he didn't puff up, I swear by God, I saw him. He didn't puff up like a fisherman's son, a fisherman's son who wanted to take a rope, hang it from a tree, and strangle himself because of what people said to him, a fisherman's son from whom Abu Saeed Al-Khudri would miss, a fisherman's son who on the day of freedom and was never seen again by anyone, this fisherman's son puffed up until he blocked the path when he got angry with Ibn 'Umar. Yes, he puffed up and until he blocked the path. Anyway, if Abu Saud did puff up, he wouldn't even block the door handle, because he is mentally weak, and I dislike him somewhat; his incompetence annoys me. I didn't express him this dislike, but there's no doubt he noticed my annoyance when he asked me to explain to him how to transfer money on the Alahli Mobile app. He didn't succeed, nor did he delete the app. I said 'money' because I just remembered that even until the sixth grade, he wouldn't say 'Riyal', saying, "Give me six money... fifty money..." Undoubtedly, this indicates a type of innocence beyond what's normal. I somewhat dislike Abu Saud because he also appears in this story as naive, ignorant, unaware of his historical context, and knows nothing about the nature of colonial economic relations. He hasn't developed an instinctive fear of American warplanes. Perhaps he did develop some of this fear, but it doesn't show in this story. By God, I don't know. Perhaps I exaggerate in all of this, or maybe a feeling of envy led me to dislike him because his demeanour is desirable. He's a good and sincere man. He worked hard until he became a radio producer. He didn't work as a presenter, he worked in production and some administrative matters, then after many nights, he became a producer. He directed programmes I didn't hear, perhaps they were good. But most likely, they were those radio programmes you listen to without knowing the producer's role. Perhaps they once hosted on their show a respected liberal thinker, very alert, who was originally a mayor, a mayor who didn't develop an instinctive fear of American warplanes. He drank the cup of tea offered to him in the studio, warm red tea infused with bergamot fruit. As he tasted the flavour of bergamot, he remembered pleasant summer days and a hazy image of a library. That night, this gentle question arose: Why didn't Atika think about making a cluster bomb? With his enthusiastic voice and his tongue, which was tinged with the scent of bergamot, and after the host interrupted him once, gesturing with his hand, the mayor narrated a poorly supported story about Atika, the daughter of Abdul Muttalib, an ordinary story, except that the thoughtful mayor cleverly inferred from it our backwardness. I found this connection very intriguing. The mayor recounted that Atika had a dream that frightened her. She saw a rider approaching on his camel until he stopped abruptly and shouted at the top of his voice, "Let's go forth, O treacherous ones, to wrestle with your opponent in three," and people gathered around him. Then he entered the mosque and the people followed him. As they surrounded him, he shouted the same words again, "Let's go forth, O treacherous ones, to wrestle with your opponent." Then he ascended with his camel to the top of Mount Abu Qubais and shouted, then he took a rock and sent it," the highly intelligent respected liberal professor repeated the word 'rock' twice or thrice and gestured with his hand, "and it came tumbling down until, at the base of the mountain, it broke up, and a piece of it entered every house in Makka." The mayor said, "These are the Arabs. These are the Arabs." The one whose mouth smelled of bergamot smiled and felt lightness and vigour because he had succeeded with this precise connection between the hurling of the rock and the cluster bomb, "This is the cluster bomb."

Atika didn't think about making a bomb like the one she saw. She was afraid of people making accusations against her. Here... we fear shame and reputation, we don't think. Then he spoke about the essence of Arabs and these words. He didn't say in every words of his that the Arabs don't understand this immense destructive power that only a coloniser needs. Do you know the story of Ahmar? Ahmar – from the Banu Adi Bin Al-Najjar tribe – killed a man from the people of Tubba Al-Yemani who had settled with them in Yathrib, so they fought, fighting them during the day and entertaining them at night. And, by God, did they entertain them at night! Well, how do you entertain someone who settled with you if you dropped upon them a bomb like the one that fell on Mr. Fuji's head in Hiroshima? Ahmar doesn't understand this desire to kill those who don't stand out to fight him, those who walk in the street and go to the grocery shop, and laugh in the evening on the river wharf. Anyway, if you asked Abu Saud about his work in radio, he wouldn't remember that show, or he might even deny it, telling you it was a magnificent programme – he often says that before all the programmes he produced on the radio. Did I say I hate Abu Saud? Maybe I exaggerated, or I was in a bad mood when I said that. Abu Saud is a good man. It saddens me that his radio programmes are not popular, but in truth, I am surprised how he hasn't developed an instinctive fear of the American warplanes since he was residing in Husain Karad's house, which was bombed and is only about 700 kilometres away from him, a distance not too far for a fighter like the Nighthawk.

B

Husain Karad, like Fadel Abbas, is an immigrant – an Iraqi immigrant. He left Iraq and settled in Germany, then Brussels, and I think in his last days he lived in New York. He slept on the street, then in a two-bedroom apartment with a shared bathroom, and once he slept in the kitchen. He read novels by Hasan Mutlak, and the novel '*Beer in the Billiards Club*' in its

English edition. And he wrote poetry: 'Gypsy Girl', 'The Night for Prophets'... etc. He ate at a restaurant run by a Hadrami named Bakran. He drinks, and when he gets drunk, he becomes delirious and pounds the ground with his foot. Before emigrating, he suffered an undiagnosed psychological disorder after seeing the bodies of the children charred in the Al-Amiriyah shelter. The Americans bombed it with a smart bomb. Yes, a smart bomb. And he thought he was somewhat lucky because their house was not damaged in the bombing that accompanied Operation Desert Storm, and neither was the cedar pencil tree standing erect in the courtyard of the house. The clothes that Mother hung in the courtyard of the house remained unaffected, but the mother's spirit was disturbed. Husain told his brother that things were getting better. His brother didn't wait, and he hanged himself on the tree. He didn't write a note, nor did he sleep. He walked with calmness and compassion, standing there looking at the clothes hanging on the line: these are Husain's trousers waving in the cold air. It was a night in February. A calm night, because the American warplanes no longer flew here. He began to gather the clothes hung on the line and arranged them on the tarp where the mother used to collect the clothes, gathering the wooden clips. He entered the house calmly. He returned amidst the darkness and the cold, with a wooden chair and a knife. With sympathy and sadness, he cut the clothesline. It was a strong and fine rope. He heard the sound of a car engine and saw a distant faint glare of its light. He didn't speak, nor did he write a letter. He looked at the family's clothes piled on the tarp, the colours of the clothes faded slightly. He noticed dust on the tarp and wiped it with his hand. He anchored the wooden chair to the ground, tied the end of the clothesline to the tree trunk, and climbed onto the chair. He extended the rope from above the branch. He tied the knot, and felt that the darkness is frustrating and the cold is heavy. He inserted his head into the noose of the knot, and secured it. Then he took his head out of the noose and descended, taking a grey wool sweater, some of whose threads had come loose, from among the clothes arranged on the tarp. The tranquillity was dense. He put on the sweater, climbed on top of the chair, inserted his neck into the noose of the knot. He wanted to think about something, but with a compassionate glance at the door of the house, then closed his eyes. The skin on his neck was flaking, he kicked a little, and died forever. His body swayed somewhat a little with the cold air, feeling neither the cold nor the density of darkness, nor hearing the crickets screech. At the call of the Fajr ritual prayer, his grandmother saw him standing, swaying, and was unsure of what she saw. She told him to come inside so he wouldn't catch a cold.

In the morning, Husain decided that he would not live in this house, the house where he saw his brother hanging from a tree. Husain, who had nothing left of his father but a watch with gold-plated iron bracelet and a suit his father wore on his wedding day, and a poor two-second footage where the father appears hesitant in a documentary about the 1991 uprising. He told his mother he would migrate, she remained silent. She sat solemnly and stayed quiet in the living room, the fan rotating above her steadily. The sunlight cascaded onto her hair, revealing the shades, emphasising the strands that appeared darker in the shade. Sisters and cousins spoke with apparent sympathy. He migrated, and I do not know if he headed towards the Saudi desert at night towards the Rafha camp, or if he went to Jordan. In those days, he ate in a restaurant managed by a Hadrami named Bakran and befriended an Egyptian from Port Said making everything easy by talking. The Egyptian from Port Said doesn't know anything about the Canberra Bombers that intended to target Almaza Airport with half a tonne of bombs but missed and hit the airport west of Cairo instead. He knows nothing about the bombers because he was born years after those incidents. Anyway, days passed for Husain Karad with a vague longing, an image of his brother, a tense noose hanging from a tree. The image never left him, even when he left the Port Said apartment and his circumstances improved somewhat, he was not reassured. An anxiety, or an old psychological disturbance associated with objects falling on a person's head. Going to school in the slender boy's company, who was dangling from pencil tree, goes to school, both returning, quarrelling, and feeling some pain in his shoulder. He didn't go anywhere with the Port Saidi. Iraqi companions attended some music performances, accompanied by Mariam and drank. He talked to her about the novel '*The Human Cockroach*' expressing his admiration for the first chapter of the story where Dostoevsky ridiculed the idea of human rationality, and drank more. He felt bitter and slow. Mariam was not impressed by him; she found him pleasant with a charming Iraqi accent. She learned the word 'zilm' from him, then left, perhaps married a Moroccan. Now, as he stretches out on the bed, he doesn't remember her. He didn't write a poem for her, wrote one for his brother instead, didn't mention the cedar pencil tree but mentioned the date palm. Once, before leaving for New York, he participated in a limited cultural activity. In New York, things for him improved a little, but just when he thought life was good, he wrote a poem about the beautiful evening and the lined green cars, about the nightclub girls, and bought an elegant suit better than the one left by his father. He decided to open a bookstore with Fadel Abbas. I tell you that when things improved slightly, and he thought life was good, the car's air conditioning broke down, and the Americans bombed their house in Iraq, his mother died, she died patiently and sad.

$$C^{1}$$

Cases recorded by Professor Frantz Fanon, a psychiatrist, describing psychiatric cases linked to French colonialism in Algeria.

Case No. 5: A European police inspector tortures his wife and children

He came to consult us of his own free will. An inspector in the police force. He noticed that for some weeks now his condition has not been normal. He is married and has three children. He smokes heavily, a hundred cigarettes a day. He has lost his appetite and experiences disturbing recurring nightmares. These nightmares do not have specific characteristics. What bothers him more than anything else is what he calls, "Fits of madness." He doesn't like anyone to contradict him; he said, "Explain to me this matter, Doctor, whenever I encounter any opposition, I feel an urge to strike. Even outside of work, I wish to punish anyone who stands in my way. Any trivial thing arouses this desire in me. For example, once I went to the newsstand to get my newspapers. There were people there,

---

1. Part 'C' is taken completely from the book: "The Wretched of the Earth" by Frantz Fanon. [The Author]

so one had to wait. I held out my arm to take my newspapers – the newsstand owner is a friend of mine – when one of the people standing in line said to me challengingly, 'Wait your turn,' I felt an urge to slap him, and I said to myself, 'If I could detain you for a few hours, my friend, you would behave better afterwards.' I can't tolerate the noise; at home, I wish I could beat up everyone in the house, all of the time. In fact, I actually did hit my, even my youngest son, who is only a year and a half old. I hit him with rare brutality. However, what I fear the most was when my wife criticised me one evening for hitting the children. She said to me, 'You've gone mad.' What I did then was to pounce on her, hitting her, then tying her to a chair. I wanted to hit her savagely, but the children started crying and screaming. That is when I realised the seriousness of the situation. I untied her and decided to consult a doctor." He said that I was not like this before, that he rarely punished his children, and never argued with his wife, and that his current behaviour manifested itself only when the current events began. He explained, "We are now engaged in street fighting. Last week, we had a fight as if we were part of the army. These gentlemen – referring to government officials – claim that there is no war in Algeria, and that the security forces, meaning the police I work with, are restoring calm to its normality, except, in Algeria, there is a war, and what particularly worries me is torture. I continue to torture sometimes for ten hours."

"What does torture do to you?"

"I get exhausted. True, there are intervals of rest for the torturers, but no one knows when to hand over the task to their colleague to complete. That's the issue with us; can you bear this man talking? It's a matter of personal triumph. We

compete, and our fists are shattered in the end. They have started to enlist the Senegalese for help. I disagree with those who
entrust the preparation of the individual to others. However,
my wife's story troubles me more than anything else. There is
no doubt that there is some madness in me that you must heal,
Doctor."

The authorities under which this patient operates refused
to grant him leave, and he does not want to obtain a certificate from a psychiatrist. Therefore, I started to treat him while
he was at work. It is clear that such a procedure is weak; the
man knew full well that his disturbances were directly related
to the type of work he was doing in the interrogation rooms,
although he tried to attribute it generally to the 'events' and did
not consider stopping the torture work — because that would
mean resigning from the police force — he asked me directly,
and without hesitation, to help him torture Algerians without
it affecting his behaviour.

The Days of Normal Life that They Talk About

Painful days pass and others return, and we never thought; we talk and forget. Those shadows moved away on rainy days. I was walking back feeling intensely bored. Maybe I was drunk — although I hadn't had a drink in any bar — or maybe the days that passed and we said wouldn't come back made my breath catch, and my thoughts became gloomy. The roads are dark, empty except for bags tossed by the wind in front of closed shops and some black silhouettes. An empty box rattles and rolls quickly. A car's red light flickered feebly. I walk on the pavement with boredom, having guessed that the rain would be heavy. The pain in my back muscles; the doctor spoke of my need for natural ivory sessions. In the morning, the sky was clear; now I see the night like accumulating ghosts without eyes. Returning, I walked on the pavement in front of some building; a furious dog barked at me, and I thought, "It will attack." I quickened my pace but didn't run. I heard a woman's voice speaking angrily, then she shut the window. I saw no one walking on the pavement, as if I were the only one returning on foot at this hour. I saw the shadow of a fat man who was originally a wild wolf. The streetlight poles shivered because the wind had intensified. The sound of rain falling on the roofs and the pavement was strong, and I was bored. I am not European and have never lived in Brussels to carry an umbrella. The intensified rain soaked my hair, the collar of my heavy coat, my shoes, and my socks. The accumulating ghosts approached, and I wanted to get there. In the narrow entrance of the building is where I stood, wanting to wait until the rain eased. The sound of a child's intermittent crying reached me. The entrance of the building was narrow and musty, and its smell was like... a man cursed at a woman[1] standing on the stairs, and then they argued as if I weren't there. I felt ashamed for I hadn't said anything, I and wanted to leave before they

---

1. It wasn't a wild wolf, nor was it a wolf caged in a zoo; he was originally a domesticated animal. She had been angry for many days because she remembered the things that hurt her soul. Then she said, "The family has made me a domesticated animal." She remembered Mother saying, "I will cut off your legs," and bringing a knife—one used for cutting yellow lemons—close to her thigh to scare her. She wet her bed again, but Mother didn't carry out her threat. When she was born, Father rejoiced, and her aunt hung balloons and colourful decorations. Mother held her, and Father photographed them with a film camera. Mother braided her hair and she entered school, studied diligently, grew up, and smoked like a young man trying to attract a girl's attention, wore makeup, fell in love with a beautiful girl, then loved the feel of smooth skin. In those days, she spoke a lot and said that Father was strict. That's why she thought about emigrating. She believed that if she changed places, the nature of the world would change. She walked with anxiety and confusion, participated in some demonstrations, until she felt confident and saw herself becoming a wild wolf.
A painful incident happened to her, in a disgusting narrow alley where cats are strong. During heavy rain, she was harassed—I'm not sure if she was raped or not—by a thin man walking, ready to steal anything. This incident caused her to experience mysterious panic attacks, and she noticed that she had become a domesticated animal. [The Author]

asked for my help. I walked under the heavy rain; the cold stung my ears and fingers. The building entrance wasn't warm like a small apartment with a heater, a bed, some food, and clean clothes, but it was better than walking on the pavement under the rain that makes the ground slippery.

I walked back, seeing the faint light of the building entrance receding. I entered a side street, the distant sound of an ambulance siren approaching, then saw the red light reflecting on the walls, the slippery ground, my face, and the palm of my hand. The sound of the ambulance siren was like the scream of the woman being pushed by a man on the stairs. My grandfather isn't bothered by the rain; he looks at the sky, rolls up his sleeves, and his spirit rejoices. The rain will not stop. Bitter delusions haunted me—had I walked down this street before? I stood, looking at the bleak, disappointing buildings to be sure, and I imagined the trees themselves walking under the rain, and if they stood in the narrow entrance of the building to avoid the heavy rain, they would find the lumberjack. I saw crows looking scornfully, as if I were the one who hunted them. I quickened my pace, and in my head, the sound of my footsteps on the pavement echoed. What is this road? Eyes watch from the windows. A woman draws the curtain, and a gentle light reaches the street from behind it. Why are the windows so small, and why do I only see wavering shadows? I'm bored, and no one is walking under the rain except me. In some window, two vile boys are looking at me. Why are they staring? Is it because the rain has soaked my coat and made it heavy? I wished I had time to beat them frightfully. I shouted at them, but they didn't notice because the glass is thick and the window is high. One of the boys was smiling and pointing at the lightning that now flashed in the sky, lighting up between the heads of the accumulating ghosts. I walked determinedly, in the side alleys, seeing shadows wavering on the buildings. I saw the shadow of a distant man warming himself by a fire, and I thought to myself, this is a doorman, and I am not a doorman. And I walked without stopping. In the building opposite, a room whose light was turned off. Under the car, a puddle of rainwater that has stopped and a cat meows in panic and looks around. I moved away from the car. In the apartment where the light was turned off, an old woman who lived through World War II and has not spoken for two days now dreams that she is in the paradise she has awaited since the end of the war. She heard that paradise would come after the fall of the Berlin Wall, and then they talked about other dates. She dreams without knowing that she will die very soon. The wind is cold and swift, and I did not think about anything because the rain was strong, and I wanted to get home to take off these wet clothes, eat, and sleep. The rain is strong and its coming down is noisy, annoying me, and it could drive me to think about death if it continues. I turned right, and my foot almost slipped. In fact, it did slip, but I didn't fall, and I don't know why I felt humiliated. I didn't recognise this street I was on. I cleaned my foot from what had stuck to it—a white adhesive paper. I walked cautiously. Ahead of me was a neighbourhood trash bin with an arsenic smell, and I felt relieved because I didn't see anyone. I turned and walked quickly, then ran to the entrance of a building. The ground was wet, and the elevator with the narrow door was not working. I heard the sound of a crying child and the rain, which had intensified anew. On the stairs, I stop to rest for a bit and look up; the coat was heavy, and I was weary. On the fifth or fourth floor, there was an apartment. I knocked on the door, a wooden door painted in dark green. I knocked again. A man[1] , half-asleep, opened the door. I asked him with my fist clenched, "Why did you hit the woman on the stairs?" He lazily replied, "I didn't hit a woman on the stairs." Then he realised and asked, "Are you the police? And what if I did hit a woman?" I told him, "I am a civilian, and you have no right to harm anyone." He grabbed my wet coat, "You are a confused sick person. Leave or I will call the police." Under his arm, I saw the shadow of an old man sleeping on a chair, and his shadow on the wall resembled… he pushed me and I said nothing. He gestured with his eyebrows and his hand, then

---

1.   This is a miserable man who never hurt anyone, but people knock on his apartment door late at night and ask him, "Why did you do such and such?" That night, a stranger came and knocked on his apartment door and asked him, "Why did you kill the woman on the stairs?" He hadn't killed his wife on the stairs. In fact, he hadn't killed her at all. She had died on the road, on one of the ordinary days of life. He was driving, travelling from one city to another, not encountering any wild animals on the way, and the road wasn't slippery because of rain. The car tyres were new, and the sun was shining, but the car overturned. He was driving fast and listening to the radio when his wife told him the baby was hungry, but he didn't hear 'hungry' because he sneezed a strong sneeze that gave him a headache. With that, the car veered off the road and overturned. Perhaps his hand hit the steering wheel; I don't know, but the car over- turned and crushed his wife's head. His wife and the hungry baby died, while he emerged from the overturned car with difficulty, disoriented, and stood shaking off his clothes. I find this a comically tragic death, fitting for the life of a man whose door people knock on for strange rea- sons. I tried to find out if the death certificate stated the cause of death as 'the husband's sneeze' or if it mentioned something medical like 'cardi- ac arrest'. But I wasn't able to find anything. Maybe one day I will also knock on his apartment door late at night and ask him about his wife's death certificate. [The Author]

closed the door. I heard him talking to someone, and when I heard him say 'the police', I remembered bitter things, which is why I didn't hit him with my clenched fist, and I said to myself, "Perhaps the woman is fortunate that he didn't chase her into the street under the rain that has intensified now." I descended the stairs without stopping or looking down. I wanted to say aloud, "Kill the woman!" because I was furious at her. I said nothing and descended quickly – he suspected that he heard the sound of a police car siren – I waited at the entrance of the building, the rain was heavy in the street. I guessed that the rain wouldn't stop and decided to leave. The rain was heavy and I felt as if someone wanted to seek revenge against me. I walked without looking at the desolate buildings, the heavy rain made things look unclear. I tried to remember the way, then entered a dirty alley. In dirty alleys, cats are stronger because they know these alleys, so I hastened, and emerged onto a wide street, with no light except at the entrances of some distant buildings. It occurred to me that I should take shelter under any of these parked cars to shield myself from the heavy rain and cold wind. However, this would be painful, and my head might get stuck in the car's fan, and it would be humiliating for me if someone found me crawling out from under the car like a hungry cat, and perhaps the owner of the car would find me and think he had found a thief and call the police. An old stone wall stood in front of me, and hadn't it been for the rain, I would have seen it from afar and turned back. I looked at the wall, then glanced at the road, unsure how I had ended up here. I climbed the wall and walked. The street, dark, and the rain, heavy. I stopped and looked up at the sky. The cold wind hurt my ears. I felt a bit lighter under the rain because I managed to overcome some obstacle. I returned to the wall and thought to myself that climbing it would be easy. I placed my foot here, then grabbed my hands and lifted my body forcefully with the strength of my arms. I climbed it and walked. I forgot where I wanted to reach; I aimed for a place with clean clothes, but I couldn't remember where the clean clothes were anymore. So, I said to myself, "I will walk on any path and not let anything stop me, not even a fierce dog guarding the entrance of the building. I will not stop." I admired this determination in myself and wanted to run through all the streets and enter all the buildings, but I felt embarrassed to be seen by someone from the window, and when I spoke, they wouldn't notice my presence. I didn't run but walked quickly. I turned right and stopped and looked. I passed by a building with windows, the rain was strong, and I continued walking. At the end of the street, a cat's shadow emerged from a trash can, a container I thought I had passed before. I walked straight and wide until I reached a dark forest; its trees seemed like crows about to pounce. Perhaps it was a cemetery or a government building, and the heavy rain made me see it as a forest. I said to myself, "I wouldn't find any clean clothes here," and I entered the forest to escape the heavy rain. I stood under the branches and large leaves. The ground was muddy, but the rain didn't wet my head or the collar of my coat. I sat down and decided to sleep here, and in the morning the rain will have stopped, and it is when the rain stops that I'll know where I wanted to go.

Very Short Stories

Why Does the Sane Soldier Think He Is a Dog?

My friend Švejk, who was written about by Jaroslav Hašek in the novel '*The Good Soldier Švejk*', who was a very good and forgiving soldier by the way, though you might think he's foolish if you don't know him beforehand. He told me that he served in World War I when he served in the 91st Infantry Regiment, if one of the soldiers fell ill – which happened often – whether they were suffering from chest infections, a lentiginous fever, gastrointestinal issues, wounded by shrapnel, exposed to mustard gas, or suffering from mental breakdowns, all these patients were committed to treatment and monitored by a veterinarian. Švejk said that. And perhaps – this is not something he said but something I imagine – the veterinarian would ask the sick soldier to bark to check his breathing or something, just as a human doctor sometimes asks a patient to cough. I don't know, I'm not a doctor anyway.

The Eerie Thoughts Triggered by Immersion in Working on the Excel Programme

While eating macaroni and observing the passing car registration plates in front of the restaurant, he pondered, without any real reason, that his existence manifests itself in his role at Budget Car Rental Company. Sometimes, after finishing a call with his mother on the landline, he thinks about being the son of a compassionate woman and tells himself, "I need to manage my finances this month to buy her the dishwasher she wishes for." But when he reads the poetic excerpts he posted on Facebook, he forgets all that and says, "I exist to be an annoyed and depressed artist. I should leave my job at Budget and pursue art, or at least work in a related field, I could work as an editor for a literary magazine." In the evening, the sound of thunder was loud. He ate a cold slice of pizza, watched a replay of a football match until he got sleepy, and still had a lot of work left in front of him on the Excel programme. At that moment, he thought he was nothing more than the dirt stuck to the whiskers of the cockroach passing in front of him right now.

A Fierce Fight about an Unspecified Topic

Yesterday, I had a terrifying dream. The wind was strong, and our feet sank into the snow. We were walking with exhaustion and fear, being driven to Nazi camps, except that there were no Nazis there; instead, armed animals were leading us. As endless groups of people, we were walking in endless lines. I saw many armed animals at checkpoints within residential areas, and other animals guarding our lines. Some were spitting on us, and some said, "Damned humans!" Walking beside me was a dog dressed in military uniform, armed with an MP40 sub-machine gun. When I asked him, "If you don't mind, where are you taking us?" he kicked me in the leg, and I stumbled. No one cared; everyone walked in submission and silence. I woke up before we reached the camp. I saw my meek dog lying next to the bed, and I felt a deep hatred towards him. When I looked into his eyes, I saw a disturbing ambiguity. I couldn't bear it; I pounced on him unconsciously and hit him with the metal lamp stand while screaming, "You want to take us to the camps, huh?" Even when he fell dead, I didn't stop. I perched over him and continued to hit his head with all the strength and blind fury I had.

Memories of the Road

When the fighting ended in the Battle of Baghdad Airport and the brutal bombardment with cluster bombs, neutron bombs, incendiary bombs, and those strange bombs dropped by the B-52s ceased, Hassoun—a language teacher who volunteered to fight in Iraq—was left sad and desperate as he fought in the battles of Al-Adhamiya. He was sad and desperate because he knew that those who survived that savage bombardment would never be considered martyrs. It occurred to him that he would die patiently waiting in his bed, like those dead, bloated donkeys he encountered on the road between Irbid and Amman.

Activities

The mother is certain that her son is doing a great humanitarian job, to the point that she once exaggerated and asked him over lunch about the number of patients whose lives he had saved. The aunt, who hopes he will marry her daughter, imagines that he spends his work hours wandering the hospital corridors looking for a suitable fiancée. The father doubted his income, saying, "He doesn't stick to his full working hours." As for him, he spends his work hours in an isolated administrative office on the third floor, sending some emails and reading the books he brings with him. From time to time, he goes out to smoke on the emergency staircase overlooking the sea, silently contemplating the calm and eternal blueness of the ocean.

The Impact of the Little Corpse on Lyudmila Usratova

When the Nazis besieged Leningrad, Lyudmila Usratova's family was also trapped. Lyudmila, this young girl of barely thirteen, when her younger brother Yurik died from starvation, she was tasked with transporting his little, delicate body on a sled, dragging it behind her to a pit specified for the burial of the dead, a mass burial. When she arrived at that pit, she saw a large truck with heaps of corpses upon it being dumped into the pit. Lyudmila stood there, waiting for them to finish. As her wait prolonged, one of the volunteers working in the burial operations asked her, "Girl, why are you standing here?" Lyudmila replied, "I am waiting for the pit to fill up so I can place my brother on top, so the burden won't be heavy on him."

This is not a story made up; I heard it from Lyudmila herself.

Family... Family... Family

When the family needed money, the father thought about selling the mother's few pieces of jewellery. The children thought the same. But the mother didn't think about selling the father's car, nor did she think about selling the children's toys. She didn't tell the father, "Stop buying cigarettes." She didn't tell him, "You are wasting money on nights out." The mother, like them, thought about selling her few pieces of jewellery. Sitting at the dining table, looking at her hand in silence, she thought that next time she wouldn't have her few pieces of jewellery to sell again.

The Skill Displayed by the Goalkeeper

In the only match where the Egyptian national team triumphed over the Italian national team—yes, the Italian team featuring Buffon, De Rossi, and Pirlo, indeed Pirlo—the Italian team that was then the World Cup champion. In that match, where the ball mysteriously stopped on the goal line of El-Hadary, the Egyptian goalkeeper. In that match, the Egyptian national team won with a goal scored by Homos—his name is Homos—his first and last goal. In that only match that ended with Egypt's victory after a barrage of missed Italian chances. In that match where Luca Toni uttered words of protest to God after squandering a clear opportunity. In that match in particular, Mr. Hassan Shehata, the coach of the Egyptian national team, stood beside the substitutes' bench. In that match where the Egyptian team won for the first and only time, Hassan Shehata was shaking, swinging his head, and sweating as if he were the one playing. In that match, whenever the ball approached the Egyptian goal and danger was imminent, Shehata, with an Egyptian accent reminiscent of a widow from Ezbet el-Nakhl, would say distressfully, "Our Master, O Messenger of Allah... My Lord, O my Beloved... O our Master the Prophet." He would clench his fists tightly and open his eyes wide anxiously, eagerly waiting until the ball moved away from El-Hadary's goal, moved far, far away.

Malaak

Look, this is a picture of Malaak, the neighbour's daughter from nearly more than seven years ago. Iraqi refugees. They moved next to us after the closure of the Rafha camp. Look at her beautiful eyes." He brushed his hand over the girl's face in the picture. "Malucha," she always tells us, after we mispronounce her name and say 'Malaak,' she responds in a stern Iraqi accent.

"My name is Malocha, not Malaak. I am six years old," and she raises five fingers, indicating her six years. Despite her young age, she was remarkably intelligent and well-mannered. When she asks my mother for food, she says, "Auntie, I want rice... Auntie, I want a spoon." She spends hours of the day with us, and hours of the night as well. She likes it when we pay attention to her and listen to her conversations, full of innocent and funny comments. She would talk about how bored she gets at mourning gatherings and say, while shaking while seated, "I want to dance, not cry." She laughed a lot and made us laugh too. After those good days, they told her about their imminent departure to Iraq. She didn't understand the reality of this until she realised that our house would not be next to theirs in Iraq, she wouldn't visit us every day, and I wouldn't crawl on all fours with her on my back. She came to us once, upset, and asked my mother if we could go with them. She said, "We won't leave you." My mother comforted her and told her it wasn't possible. We bade her farewell with false promises, "We will visit you in Iraq." After they left, contact with them was lost, until one joyous afternoon, we received a call on the landline, "This is Malucha, I'm calling you from Samarra," with a voice filled with laughter. We talked to her for a long time. Her happy calls continued until we moved from our house, and we left the phone number for the new owner, or perhaps my father cancelled the number, I don't remember.

Today, as I look at her picture, I thought about the number of times Malucha might have called the old number and no one answered, and she didn't get to say with a laughing voice, "This is Malucha, I'm calling you from Samarra."

Modern Day Dogs

Dog, I am a dog, yet I am not like those dogs that snarl and bark at a strange face. Or those fierce ones that work with the police in films. Or those uncouth dogs that want to roam and bark with joy. I am from those hesitant dogs, from those dogs that are afraid to bark, from those dogs that think about the consequences. I am from those dogs that, if they entered the henhouse, the hens would peck at them.

Interruptions in Laughter

In those days, I used to play with the children and mimic the sound of the wolf poorly, then I would attack them while they jumped around me laughing, and their little eyes sparkled like real sheep. Since I became a government employee receiving a monthly salary, I contemplate a lot and remain silent, as if the wolf has died.

The Colour of Iron Filings

In a distant time, in the days of childhood, the Tapline pipes accompanied us all along the way. These rusty red pipes were companions of the wild adventures; in places where they approached the ground, we competed in jumping over them, and in places where they rose above the ground, we competed in walking on them. We threw stones at them, sat on them like a knight a horse, and wiped our hands on them not seeking blessings, but to take on their red colour, the colour of rusty iron filings. We pressed our ears against them to imagine the sound of the oil flowing through, which had ceased pumping. Once my mother told me that the pipes stretch all the way to Lebanon. It was a strange idea, Lebanon, where is Lebanon? Since that moment, whenever we stopped to play on the Tapline pipes, I would take a medium-sized stone and move away until the sounds of the family faded, then I would hit the iron of the Tapline pipe with all my strength, two or three consecutive knocks, and press my ear against the iron, waiting to hear the response that might come from a boy in faraway Lebanon. No response ever came, I would only hear the ringing of my knocks, and my cheeks would take on red colour, the colour of iron filings.

He Who Keeps Our Goal

My mother doesn't know much about football, but when she finds out that the team is playing, she asks me about Mohamed Al-Deayea, "Is he playing with them or not?" so she can pray for them. She says, "I feel sorry for him because his build is skinny, and I don't want him to lose," – she thinks he doesn't eat well. My mother doesn't know that this boy, with his thin build and two gloves, stopped Frank Rijkaard and Dennis Bergkamp. "This boy, Mom, with the courage of Al-Haili and his spontaneity, used to tell the team, "Attack and leave the goal to me." And they would do it, leaving the goal to him alone, Mom."

ABOUT THE AUTHOR

Mohammed Al-Aradi, a Saudi writer born in 1987, began writing short stories in 2010, publishing them on literary internet platforms, newspapers, magazines, and literary journals. He dedicated ten years to short story writing before selecting a collection of works from that period and publishing his first short story collection, *Why Does the Sane Soldier Think He's a Dog?*, in 2020, released by Kalemat Publishing House. He later published his second short story collection, *The Anxiety of Missed Opportunities*, in 2024, also under Kalemat Publishing House.

www.ingramcontent.com/pod-product-compliance
Lightning Source LLC
Chambersburg PA
CBHW021018180626
46814CB00003B/1345